Henry Clifford

The life of Jane Dormer

Duchess of Feria

Henry Clifford

The life of Jane Dormer
Duchess of Feria

ISBN/EAN: 9783741189197

Manufactured in Europe, USA, Canada, Australia, Japa

Cover: Foto ©Raphael Reischuk / pixelio.de

Manufactured and distributed by brebook publishing software
(www.brebook.com)

Henry Clifford

The life of Jane Dormer

Quarterly Series

SIXTY-SECOND VOLUME

THE LIFE OF THE DUCHESS OF FERIA

THE LIFE OF JANE DORMER
DUCHESS OF FERIA

BY

HENRY CLIFFORD

Transcribed from the Ancient Manuscript in the possession of the Lord Dormer

BY THE LATE

CANON E. E. ESTCOURT

AND EDITED BY THE

REV. JOSEPH STEVENSON
OF THE SOCIETY OF JESUS

LONDON
BURNS AND OATES
LIMITED
GRANVILLE MANSIONS W
1887

PREFACE.

THE following pages contain an interesting sketch of the life of Jane Dormer, Duchess of Feria, extending from the time of her birth during the reign of king Henry the Eighth to that of her death in the reign of James the First. It contains many interesting details respecting the personal character and social condition of various individuals with whom it is instructive to become thus familiarly acquainted. Its author commands at once our attention and our confidence by reminding us of his own personal knowledge of most of the incidents which he has here recorded. He was an inmate of the family of the Duchess; he had resided for many years in her household; he possessed her confidence, he witnessed her death and assisted at her funeral. We feel that we may trust his statements without hesitation. He writes with a quiet simplicity which recommends what he has here chronicled ; and we gladly, accept his story, homely as it is, as more than a compensation for that lack of artistic skill which the reader cannot fail to detect in the structure of the following narrative.

Our chronicle opens with a sketch of the history of the noble family of Dormer, the accuracy of which, in some of its earlier details, may possibly be questioned. But the attention of the reader is speedily arrested by the precious details with which it furnishes him respecting the life, sufferings and death of Father Sebastian Nudigate, who takes his place along with Cardinal Fisher and Sir Thomas More among the noble army of martyrs who died for the faith under Henry the Eighth.[1] Several interesting particulars as to the private character and domestic virtues of Queen Catharine of Aragon next claim our notice. We learn that she rose at midnight to

[1] P. 19.

be present at the Matins of the Religious, after which she heard Mass at five o'clock in the morning. Under her royal attire she wore the habit of St. Francis, "having taken the profession of his Third Order." She fasted on bread and water every Friday and Saturday, and on all the eves of our Blessed Lady, whose Office she read daily. On every Sunday she received the Blessed Sacrament of the Altar. Most part of her morning was spent in the Church at holy Service, and after dinner she read the life. of the Saint of the day to her maids. And then she returned to the Church. She was banished from the Court to Kimbolton, where it was said that her days had been shortened by the unwholesome air, while some were of opinion that poison had been administered, "for the lady Anne hated her extremely."[2]

Of Anne Boleyn a few characteristic sketches are preserved. Her life was very different to that of her predecessor, being passed chiefly in masks, plays, dancing and such personal de-

[2] P. 73-78.

lights, "in which she had a special grace." Our author has preserved a story, which he believed to be true, of Anne having attempted to poison Cardinal Fisher; and he states that the agent in the plot "being discovered did confess it and was publicly put to death for it." Several other reports of a kindred nature follow; which, be they true or false, show the estimation in which Anne's morality was generally regarded by her contemporaries.[8]

Edward the Sixth next claims at once our attention and our sympathy. In order that the new doctrine now introduced into England might take the deeper root, we are told that apostate priests and friars from foreign parts, with their wives, were entertained in this kingdom, and sent to be public preachers in the Universities, where they taught heresies. If any pious or learned Catholic gainsaid (as many did) the doctrine of these outlandish apostates, they were persecuted, put to silence, deprived of their livings, imprisoned, or banished. The calm firmness with which this iniquitous

[8] P. 76–85.

attempt was resisted by a considerable number of the English people is well illustrated by the account here given of the conduct of the Princess Mary and the family of the Dormers.

Of the little Prince himself some pleasing reminiscences are here recorded, and they come to us in a form which commands our acceptance. Our Biographer writes as follows. " I have heard them that were about the Prince avouch it, that his inclination was of great towardness to all virtuous parts and princely qualities. He was a marvellous sweet child, of very mild and generous condition. Afterwards when his father died (he being but nine years of age) mischievous and heretical governors, contrary to his father's will, abused his tender age; who ruling to effect their own ends notoriously injured the natural good inclinations of this gentle and noble prince. For, when he was king, in passing by the ruins of goodly monasteries, he demanded what buildings were these; it was answered, that they were religious houses, dissolved and demolished by order of the king his father for

a 2

abuses. Edward replied; "Could not my
father punish the offenders and suffer so goodly
buildings to stand, and put in better men that
might have governed and inhabited them?"
seeming to lament that lamentable course."

From the same authority we learn that the
Princess Mary, having gained some influence
over the little Edward, order was taken by his
tutors that the visits of his half-sister should be
very rare, upon the plea that they made him
unhappy and melancholy. It was intended also
that proceedings should have been taken against
Mary's officers and servants for violating the
newly made law, she having had public Mass in
her chapel; but Edward refused to sanction this
prosecution, and strictly commanded that the
Princess should have full liberty to follow the
dictates of her conscience.[4]

The accession of Elizabeth was a turning-point
in the history of Jane Dormer. During the reign
of Queen Mary her sister, the Princess Elizabeth
had professed herself to be a zealous Catholic,
and as such had deliberately practised the duties

[4] P. 61, 62.

required by the Church; but when she found herself safely mounted on the throne of England, she appeared before the world in her true character. The marriage of Jane Dormer to the Count de Feria, Philip's trusted minister, rendered her residence in England no longer possible; and accordingly she bid farewell to the land of her birth, never to return. Her parting interview with Elizabeth and her journey through Flanders and France on her way to her new home in Spain, are here recorded with some minuteness; among the more interesting details of which may be specified the pleasing glimpse which it affords us of the visit which she paid to Mary Stuart, at that time Queen of France and wife of king Francis the Second.

We cannot find space to trace step by step the account here given of the life of the Duchess of Feria during the years which she spent in Spain. In every capacity in which we meet her she appears to advantage; as wife, as mother and as widow; at home and abroad; as mistress of a large household, amidst the temptations of a brilliant court; in her domestic relations with the society with which she mingled, and in her public and private devotions. Just and prudent as well as kindly and generous, she seems to have won the confidence and secured the affections of all with whom she came into contact. While we wish that the narrative of her biographer had been somewhat more diffuse upon certain particulars, we are grateful to him for the details which, but for his loving care would have perished. We treasure the lessons which her example teaches us. Henceforward the name of Jane Dormer, Duchess of Feria, takes its place in our memory as one of that company of good women of which Catholic England has cause to be proud; and we here cordially thank the present noble inheritor of her Name and her Creed, for the privilege of at length becoming acquainted with the virtues of his illustrious ancestress.

And now a few words must be devoted to the insufficient details which have come down to us respecting the author of the following narrative.

The little which we know about the history of Henry Clifford, the biographer of the Duchess of Feria, is derived from the Dormer manuscript.

This narrative, as it stands at the present time, was written in the year 1643, and it was then presented by the author to Charles Dormer, Earl of Carnarvon and Lord Baron of Wing; but it had evidently been drawn up at a much earlier date, while the incidents which are here recorded were fresh in the memory of the narrator. In the Preface to the Life of the Duchess, as we now have it, Clifford tells us that he had derived his information partly from what he himself had seen, known and heard; and partly from the information of trustworthy authorities. From the way in which he mentions an incident which occurred at Oxford when he was a boy there in 1581 or 1582, we may infer that he was born somewhere about the year 1570.[5] He must have been in the service of the Duchess for some time before 1605, for in that year she bestowed upon him an annuity of twenty pounds, as well as the sum of forty pounds due to the Lady Hungerford, lately deceased.[6] He had received information respect-

---

[5] See the present volume, p. 38.

[6] She died 19th December, 1603. See Clifford's letter to Sir Robert Dormer, dated Madrid, 14th December, 1605.

ing the duchess from the Earl of Nottingham, who had seen her when he was ambassador in Spain in 1605.[7] But at this period Clifford had been for some time in the service of the duchess and had secured her confidence, as will appear by the extracts which will presently be given from his correspondence. The narrative was in process of composition, or perhaps of final revision, in 1616.[8] From these indications we may venture to believe that it was begun very shortly after the death of the Duchess of Feria, which occurred on 23rd January, 1613.[9]

During the course of the narrative its author mentions circumstances which shew that he held an official position in the ducal household, and one moreover which brought him into frequent and confidential intercourse with its head. By the duchess he was made acquainted with some conversation of a private nature which had passed between herself and her husband.[10] We have already seen that he was in her service in 1605, at which time he occupied

---

[7] P. 68.   [8] P. 8.

[9] P. 200.   [10] P. 132.

a situation of trust and authority.[11] He was
in close attendance upon her during her
last sickness;[12] he stood by her deathbed in
company with two Fathers of the Society of
Jesus, four Franciscan Friars, one Dominican
and her chaplain;[13] and as she drew her last
breath she put into his hands the rosary which
she had used, "on which she meditated and had
often discoursed."[14] And as the highest token
of their respect for his services, her family
entrusted him with the arrangement of her
funeral, of the details of which he has left us a
full account in the concluding pages of his narrative.

The Manuscript at Grove Park which has
furnished the Biography of the Duchess of Feria
also contains copies of several letters addressed
by Henry Clifford to Sir Robert Dormer
(created Baron Dormer of Wing in 1615) the
following extracts from which will be read with
interest.

---

[11] Pp. 154, 155. See also the extracts from his letters written
at this time to Sir Robert Dormer.

[12] Pp. 185, 189.　　　[13] P. 192.　　　[14] P. 181.

Madrid, 8th October, 1605.

"I thank God her Grace for her health passeth reasonable well, although troubled often with such infirm and diseaseful accidents as her age is subject unto.

Of the duke of Feria his letters intended for England, as I remember, I certified in my last, and am glad they be received. It argues his honorable disposition that finding by those things he shall receive from you, and from hence, the antiquity and nobility that he hath in his blood from his mother will bind that love and respect which so near affinity requires.

On the 23rd of July there died in Valladolid Sir Thomas Palmer, a Western knight. I think he was of the king's Privy Chamber. His sickness was the small-pox. He died a Catholic and very Christianly."

Madrid, 14 December, 1605.

"If you have not the pedigree ready I pray trouble yourself no further in it, for I shall make a perfect one here, having both the descents by Dormer and Sydney, with their arms and matches,

under Clarencius' hand, as in part you may perceive by this note translated, which I wrote in
Latin for the duke. And when I have finished
the draft as I have devised and her Grace desireth,
against the truth of which no exception shall be
taken, I will send you a copy; wherein you
shall see your house allied with all the great
houses of Christendom. Of the Herald's errors
in the Pedigree you sent I noted in my last,
which were much mistaken.

Her Grace passeth with her health in reasonable sort; and I hope by God His preservation I
shall serve her yet very many years."

Madrid, 22nd March, 1606.

"I thank God her Grace passeth with indifferent
health and beareth her age reasonably well, for on
Twelfth day last she made fully seventy-one years
of age, and yet hath her discretion, judgment and
memory as mature as ever; and you would won-
der to hear how well she discourses in her own
language, with such fit terms and good words as
such English as came hither to visit her marvel
at it; seeing since she left England the language

hath been much altered and refined. But above all her great virtue and admirable example of modest and matron-like carriage give her the honour of all the ladies I know, and without flattery may term her the mirror of her sex and honour of our nation. She hath been widow almost these thirty-eight years [15] and with those remarkable parts of recollection and notable Christianity that all that know her give her much respect and reverence."

Madrid, 17th January, 1609.

"Her Grace (I thank God) enjoys reasonable health, although her many years and the absence of the duque her son, and somewhat the affectionate desire she hath to see your house advanced, deprive her of much contentment; and if she were partaker of these latter she should pass the former with much more ease and comfort.

Yet, sir, if you did know her memory, her discourse, her government, having the management of all her son's estate, the labours that she taketh, rising with the day and presently entering into her oratory, where she remains two

[15] But see p. 129 of the present volume.

hours. Then her chaplain comes to say Mass, which ended, if it be a Feast day she goes to church, as every day she does this Holy Week before Easter. If not she disposeth herself to such affairs as are offered. Ever if she have health, in business, for her diet (which is very temperate) keeps the English order, at eleven o'clock, or soon after. In the afternoon commonly she visits, or is visited, by other ladies; but never goeth to sleep before she hath ended her office and ordinary devotions, which are many. You would say she were not only the great honour of her house but the glory of her country; and herein she shews herself to be truly the daughter of your noble grandmother, who shewed herself a lady of worthy example in all nobility and piety."

One more interview with the good duchess and we bring these introductory remarks to a conclusion.

In the year 1596, James the Sixth, king of Scotland, sent an embassy into Spain, under Robert, fourth lord Simpill, to congratulate king Philip the Third on his accession to the throne. The ambassador while at the Court became acquainted with the Duchess of Feria, whose letter to the king (dated at Madrid, 3rd June, 1600,) has been preserved in the Advocates Library at Edinburgh.[16] She reminds him of the dutiful affection which she bore to that blessed queen his mother, as also of the honour which she bears to his Majesty; in whom if she might also see her zeal in the Catholic religion, she professes she would be bounden to God for the hope she would receive by him for the repair of her wracks, both spiritual and temporal. She concludes with these words: "Wherefore I cease not to beseech daily the Almighty to illuminate your Majesty in that behalf, and to make you as great a saint on earth as was your blessed mother, to the advancement of His glory and good of our country."

Under the same date the duchess forwarded to King James certain "Reasons to intimate to the king's Majesty of Scotland whereby it may appear that his best way to obtain the crown of England is to become Catholic, and to give

[16] Numbered, MS. 33, 1, 10.

satisfaction thereof to the Catholics of England."

She premises that in England there are three sorts of men of different profession, namely, Catholics, Heretics and men of no religion, she continues her argument by remarking: that of these the "Catholics exceed in number either of the others; and of the three the zealous heretics are the most fervent; for the greatest part of all those that live in obedience to the Queen's laws are either dissembling Catholics or men of no religion, who would be as ready to follow a Catholic prince as an heretic, if occasion served."

So then, argued the duchess, if the King's Majesty of Scotland gained the Catholics, he consequently would gain the greatest part of those that are indifferent, or of no religion. For although some of them may be moved with particular affection to some pretender within the realm, yet the greater number of them will ever follow the strongest, which no doubt will be the king's Majesty of Scotland if the Catholics adhere to him; the other pretenders being divided amongst themselves.

The paper concludes with the following words of caution. "The Catholics, having noted His Majesty's education in heresy, his many actions conform to the same, the small satisfaction that he hath given to such as have sought his conversion, ascribe his moderate course used hitherto rather to policy than to any good inclination to the Catholic Faith. Therefore they cannot but think it dangerous to the Church of God and themselves to advance his title except they have assurance of his sincerity in religion; so that in the state that His Majesty now standeth, he cannot make any assured account to have any sufficient party in England." [17]

The text of the Life of the Duchess of Feria which forms the basis of the present volume was prepared for the press some years ago by the late Rev. E. E. Estcourt, Canon of St. Chad's Cathedral, Birmingham; who also at considerable expense collected a large amount of valuable material, illustrative of the incidents, persons and places which are mentioned in the narra-

---

[17] On Sempil's mission to Spain, see some additional details in Burton's History of Scotland, v. 286, ed. 1876.

tive.[19] The long illness and untimely death of the learned Canon prevented the appearance of his intended work in the form which had originally been announced. Now at length, after the delay of many years, the biographical narrative, as prepared by Canon Estcourt, is here issued by the present editor; but he has unwillingly been compelled to omit the many illustrative papers, pedigrees, drawings and other supplementary matter which had been brought together by the research and industry of the original Editor. The biography of the duchess as prepared by him for the press is here printed from his own transcript; and this little volume is now given to the public by the present Editor as a tribute to one whose loss he laments and whose memory he cherishes.

JOSEPH STEVENSON, S.J.

12th September, 1887.

---

[19] Here the present Editor cannot refrain from mentioning the existence at Grove Park of two admirable portraits of the Duchess of Feria. The first represents her as a young woman, in the pride of her beauty, and arrayed in all the splendour of the Court of Spain. In the second she appears in the plain and severe religious habit which she assumed on the death of her husband, and which she continued to wear during the remaining years of her widowhood.

AUTHOR'S PREFACE.

TO THE RIGHT HONOURABLE HIS HONOURABLE
GOOD LORD, CHARLES DORMER, EARL OF
CARNARVON AND LORD BARON OF WING.

This treatise hath long lain by me, having dedicated it to your honourable great-grandmother, my lady the Lady Elisabeth Dormer, of happy memory. But it having pleased Almighty God to take her to a better world, where she enjoyeth the reward of her virtuous life and her many good works, I did then present it to your most noble and valiant father, who in the penning of this Epistle died, to his eternal honour and valour, in the service of his prince at the battle of Newbury, this year 1643, professing his happiness and content to die in the confession of the Roman Catholic faith and performance to his duty to his lawful king and sovereign. Your Lordship

B

being kin of his house, and in confidence of his virtue and valour, I should have forgotten my duty, to have intituled it to any other, seeing the Lady Jane Dormer, Duchess of Feria, whose life and death it chiefly handleth, being so singular and renowned an honour to your noble family, and sister to my Lord Dormer your honourable great-grandfather.

In her Excellency your Lordship will behold a lively mirror of true Nobility, christian Piety, and illustrious Honour, an eternal worthy Pattern to your House and Posterity. In this treatise is also touched, as the course of the history occasioned, the the life of her virtuous Grandmother, the Lady Jane Dormer, and of her Saint-Brother, a Carthusian martyr, both of blessed memory; of the Lady Hungerford, Sister to my Lady Duchess; the life of the most excellent and pious Queen, Queen Mary, her Lady and Mistress; and the lives of both the Dukes, her husband and son. What is written here is out of approved histories, or from the relation of such persons against whose worth and credit no exceptions may morally be given; or from that which I myself have known, seen and heard. For my purpose and intention is to tell truth. To flatter, is either to gain, or to deceive; this is of vile and base negociants, the other of shifters and lewd companions, as Plutarch saith, the infamy of free men and custom of slaves. Extreme is the folly to use fiction where there is no necessity nor occasion; and to illustrate the honour and worth of so renowned and holy a personage with untruths, I hold it sacrilege; and to deprive her of right and due were apparent injury.

This history deserves a better and more learned pen; but I trust your Lordship will pardon defects, and accept in good part my good will in performing the duty, and obligation I owe to the happy memory of my most honourable good Lady and Mistress; and the serviceable respect and love I bear to your most noble House and Family, and in particular to your Lordship, whose life, health and happiness, may God Almighty bless with that prosperous increase of honours; as desireth your Lordship's most humble and affectionate servant,

H. CLIFFORD.

The Life of the Lady Jane Dormer, Duchess of Feria.

CHAPTER I.

THE DESCENT AND BIRTH OF THE LADY JANE DORMER.

THE Lady Jane Dormer was born of parents, whose progenitors have been of the most ancient nobility of England, and of worthy esteem, both in descent of blood, and effects of valour and virtue. The Cardinal Nicholas de Peleve, Archbishop of Rheims, and first Peer of France, well understood this, when, in the name of the Three Estates of that Kingdom, he answered the oration of the Duke of Feria, her son, who was Ambassador from Philip II. 2nd April, in the year 1593, to the League at Paris. "I cannot refrain," said the Archbishop "from mentioning your Mother,

who descended from the most illustrious Families
of England, daily bestows her bounty to relieve
and cherish the afflicted exiles for religion in
Spain, who are English, Irish, and Scots."

The family of Dormer, (as I have seen in an
old Pedigree, which is confirmed by tradition),
was anciently seated in Normandy, at the time
when King Edward the Confessor took refuge
there from the tyranny of Harold Harefoot, son
of King Canute, who had usurped the kingdom.
On being recalled from Normandy by Harold's
successor, Hardicanute, Prince Edward brought
in his retinue Thomas D'Ormer among other
Norman gentlemen, all of whom he advanced to
great places and dignities. The old tradition
saith, that in the wars which King Edward had
with the Danes and with Earl Godwin he was
much assisted with monies, which the said
Thomas D'Ormer lent him. And after a success-
ful end of these wars D'Ormer invited the King
to his house to dinner; which done, he brought
the tallies in a dish that were evidences of the
money which he had lent to the King, saying,
that for the hononr done his house, he had no
better dish to show his thankfulness withal, than
these wooden chips; and so he cast the tallies in-

to the fire. The King understood by the number of the tallies the value of his debt, and the greatness of the gift, replied, with allusion to the Etymology of his name, " Well mayst thou be called D'Ormer, thou hast a sea of gold, doing what thou hast done." In memory whereof it is said, the Arms of Dormer were altered; for whereas they formerly were a lion rampant, sable, on a gold field, there was added, Azure, ten gold Billets, and the lion placed in chief.[1]

Some may object, that neither the name of Thomas Dormer, nor any such act of service is found mentioned in any history; and that at that time the usage had not begun of bearing arms to distinguish families. But Stow in his English Chronicle (p. 94.) recordeth, that King Edward brought many out of Normandy, whom he promoted to divers dignities, but nameth only two, who were Churchmen. And of the many, why might not Thomas Dormer be one? And in memory of this service of Thomas Dormer to his King, some succeeding Prince might grant his arms to be honoured, as it is; divers Kings having done the

[1] Clifford here cites as his authority " P. Ribadeneyra in su Epistola del libro de los Santos Estravagantes, dedicada a la duquesa de Feria."

like to the posterity of them, who by their noble exploits have well-merited of their country.

The son of this Thomas was William D'Ormer, who joined with the Normans his countrymen, when King William invaded England. His son was likewise William, whose genealogy, in the heir male hath continued in lawful succession to this year 1616. The Lord Dormer that now lives, being the only brother of the said Duchess of Feria, among whose ancestors was Sir William Dormer, who valiantly served King Edward the Third in his wars against France about the year 1350. Another, Geoffrey Dormer, in King Henry the Sixth his days, had twenty-six children, and most of them sons. But for the particulars of progenitors, it is not my purpose to rehearse, but only to discourse of such as were concerned in the birth, education, and life of the said Jane Dormer.

Robert Dormer, who was afterwards Sir Robert, the grandfather of our Lady Duchess, married Jane the daughter of John Nudigate of Harefield in Middlesex, and Dame Amphyllis Nevill of the house of Westmoreland. This Sir Robert Dormer, a chief man of his country, a great housekeeper, was beloved and honoured of

his neighbours. He was called by King Henry
VIII. to be Treasurer of his army, wherewith
the King went himself to Motterell in France.
He was so beloved that the King, respecting
his worth and valour, would have kept him at
his court; but he returned into England
voluntarily, retired to his house. Here he
was contented to live among his neighbours,
as his ancestors had done before him. For
in those times good men of hospitality rather
fled than followed high and ambitious titles.
A further cause of his absence from the Court
was first, the power and ambition of such as
commanded, and afterwards, the King's disorder
in questioning the lawful marriage with his
good and virtuous wife Catharine. Proceeding
to worse, came the grief that good Catholic
men took for his departure from the obedience
of God's Church, together with his violent
persecution of such as constantly remained
in the profession thereof; wherein this good
knight shewed his zeal to God His truth.
For when he saw the course and purpose of
the King in his Parliament to carry all matters
according to his passion, (which to crop or
gainsay menaced utter ruin) he avoided by all

means to be a Parliament man; for being
chosen by his County to be Knight of the
Shire, he refused it and resigned it over to
another, persuading the County that so it was
best for them. And when the King by Act of
Parliament took into his possession Abbey-
lands, which to make more plausible, in winning
the approbation of his subjects to this unchristian
act, Sir Robert gave to divers the said lands,
or sold them for little or nothing in respect of
their value; and offered to many gentlemen, of
living and regard in their countries, such lands
at a very low price, in a sort forced them to
take them. This he did, for if they denied or
shrunk back, suspicion was presently taken of
their aversion from the King in this Act; and
they came in danger to be questioned for their
allegiance. This Knight sought by all possi-
bilities, to avoid the buying of any such lands,
which had been bestowed to the service of
Almighty God.

This being noted by some about the King,
they gave information to his Majesty to incense
him against Sir Robert Dormer, thereby to
question both his life and living. So by per-
suasion of friends, he was in a sort compelled

to buy Abbot's Aston, a manor not far from his
house. In lieu whereof, his house was a refuge
and entertainment to all distressed and persecuted Catholics, both priests and others, who
retired themselves not to subscribe to this
unheard of tyranny of a christian king.

With the like hospitality and works of charity,
this good Knight did pass the time that he lived
in King Edward's reign; who by no means
either by importunity, by threats, or by other
devices, could be brought to follow, flatter, or
yield to the disordered desires of those who
governed in that child-king's days. For Sir
Robert's son, having but two daughters, the
Lady Jane and her sister, then in appearance
to be heirs of his large domains, (their Father
remaining a widower nine years,) they were
sought by the greatest to be matched to the next
of their blood. But the old discreet knight,
albeit for the present their authority was mighty
and pretending shelter under their shadows, yet
doubting the fall would be as sudden of such
high climbers, or some unhappy result of ambition without religion or respect to God's service,
could not be induced to hearken to those motions,
choosing rather to have those young gentle-

women, the wives of gentlemen of christian
integrity, than of great ones, who were stained
with the foul spots of such ungodly carriage.
For to this end the Duke of Northumberland
himself came once to his house of purpose to
propound a match for one of his sons, and to
make Sir Robert Dormer, (much beloved in his
country,) a sure friend for his designs; but
prevailed not.

This good knight, full of good works and
zealous of God's honour, changed this mortal
life for the immortal, in the year 1552; leaving
the Lady Jane his widow, with whom he had
lived forty years. It was she who was the
bringer-up of her granddaughter, the Lady Jane;
and was really more noble by her virtue and
sanctity of life, than by birth, though descended
of the Nevills of the royal house of Lancaster.
She was grandchild to Sir John Nevill, her
mother being his daughter and heir; and thus
was descended of Thomas Nevill and Anne his
wife, who was daughter to John Holland, Duke
of Exeter, and Elisabeth his wife, the daughter
of John of Gaunt.

The mother of Jane Dormer was the Lady
Mary Sidney, eldest daughter of Sir William

Sidney, Governor and High Chamberlain of
Prince Edward in the time of King Henry VIII.
his Father; one of the heirs of Charles Brandon,
Duke of Suffolk, being his cousin german.

Her brother was Sir Henry Sidney, who
married Mary, daughter of the Duke of Northumberland, and was Lord Deputy of Ireland
eight years. His daughter was the Countess of
Pembroke, mother of Sir Philip Sidney.

Of Sir Henry's other sisters one married the
father of the Lord Harrington; the third Sir
William Fitzwilliams. The youngest, Frances,
married the Earl of Sussex, Lord Chamberlain
to Queen Elizabeth, and was the foundress of
Sidney Sussex College in Cambridge. There
were other two sisters, who died unmarried;
both served the Lady Mary before she was
Queen, and were much beloved by her for their
rare virtue, and zeal in Catholic Religion.

Sir William Dormer by this his former wife
had but these two daughters, Jane the subject of
these memoirs, and Anne married to the Lord
Hungerford. By his latter wife he had a son
and three daughters, his son the now Lord
Dormer, married Elisabeth, daughter of Antony,
Viscount Montagu, and Magdalen his wife,

daughter of the Lord Dacre of the North, through whom he allied his house with many noble families.

Sir William's eldest daughter by this wife was married to the son aud heir of the Viscount Montague, and is mother of Antony the now Viscount, a very Catholic and religious nobleman. His second daughter, Catharine, married the Lord St. John of Bletstoe; and his youngest daughter, Margaret, to Sir Henry Constable of the North, a very ancient and noble gentleman, whose son is the present Viscount of Dunbar, and married the sister of the Countess of Rutland.

CHAPTER II.

JANE DORMER was born at Ethrop, not far from
Aylesbury in the County of Buckingham, in her
grandfather's house, on the 6th of January, the
year of our Lord 1538, being Sunday, and the
Feast of the Epiphany; therein presaging the
virtues of her after life by coming into the world,
when Christians were rejoicing in the birth of
our Lord.

In her baptism the name of Jane was given to
her after her grandmother; and this name signifying grace, how well it did befit her will appear
in her life. When she began to speak and
discern, and learn her duty, her natural inclinations might easily be seen. She was apt, very
disciplinable, obedient, humble, awful, generous
in her condition; so that she seemed a child only
in years. She was much beloved by the servants

and gentlewomen, that were in her grandmother's house, (for there were many of noble descent, commended by their parents, to learn good education and virtue in that house), all presaging, that so sweet conditions, in so tender years and so graceful a countenance, gave hope to produce answerable effects. So obedient a child was she to her parents and so subject to her tutress, as shewed plainly her good disposition and marvellous towardness. She was very forward to kneel upon her knees, to bless herself, to learn her prayers, to delight to go to the chapel, to have books and beads in her hands; and very prompt with contentment to all holy things. When she came to the age of four years, it pleased God to take her mother out of this world; that in her infancy the child might begin to taste the troubles and inconstancy of the world by so great a loss in a tender age. Her grandmother then took upon her the charge of bringing her up, and she was so rare and worthy a matron, there were few like her; of whose life and notable actions I shall record something.

The Lady Jane, daughter of John Nudigate, was married to Sir Robert Dormer in the year 1512. Of this marriage was born only one son,

Sir William. Before her marriage she was a mirror of recollection and devotion; as a wife, of modesty, prudence, and charity; as a widow, of patience, piety, and holy exercises. She was always a great friend of integrity; an enemy to vanity, very humble, severe to herself, fervent towards God, full of pity and compassion to the poor, and ever gracious and charitable to her neighbours and tenants. If any was sick, they were assured of her care and were cherished with good meats, and what else was necessary. Not only did she send daily to visit them, but she did not leave to see them herself, and succour their necessities; especially women in childbed. Even the poorest neighbour would she comfort with her presence, and with liberal hand she relieved them.

Such was the entire, chaste and true affection, wherewith she honoured and observed her husband, as she hath been known to affirm, that if he had died the very day of their marriage, she would never have married again. Such was her prudence, that he referred to her the government of his house and estate, which all his life she governed with great discretion and notable moderation. She brought up her son to fear God,

c

she so ordered her family, so took account of her
servants, and had care that all did their duty, as
it seemed that she had set before her eyes for her
guide and example the portraiture of "the valorous woman" painted by King Solomon. Always
she had a special eye to her maid-servants, that
they should keep home, be modest, shamefaced,
honest in behaviour. Her whole life praised her
memory. Herein were everywhere seen her
usual alms to the poor; her great charity to
priests, religious, and other distressed persons,
whom the impiety of the time persecuted; her
continual hospitality; her zealous counsels, and
Christian admonitions to her kin and friends
to persevere in the Catholic Faith; and her
care and diligence to remove from them all
hindrances, that might cool this perseverance.
Her women servants were relieved with honest
portions, some to marry, others to enter into
religion. Here too should be noted her accustomed bounty to the Church for the advancement
of God's service; her own labour and the labours
of her servants to work vestments, altar cloths,
and other ornaments for the same; her devotion
and fervour to the Catholic Religion in the time
of schism and apostacy by sustaining priests, not

only for her own house, but for the assistance
and comfort of her neighbours; her hate of
heresy; her hours spent in prayer and recollection; her works, her words;—all these things
praise her and record her memory.

This Lady's brother, Sebastian Nudigate, was
a gentleman of good parts, and of the Privy
Chamber to King Henry the VIII., and not a little
favoured by him. This king too much carried
with his lustful appetites, began to be weary of
his virtuous wife, and sensually to affect others.
Hereupon this good Lady Dormer, fearing lest
the bad example of so great a king should also
corrupt her brother, invited him to her house,
(which they make ordinarily a day's journey from
London); discoursed with him of the alteration
of the court; what was bruited in the country of
the dissolute behaviour of the Courtiers; and the
infamous example of the king, in rejecting so
famous, noble and virtuous a Lady as the Queen
was. She advised him to take heed of the
deceits of the world, and the snares of the devil;
to look to the duty of a Christian; and not to
stain his soul and honour with so dangerous and
pestilent contagions, as the bad example of so
potent a master did lead him to. He replying,

excused the king his master by saying that the
report and her opinion of the king were worse
than he demerited; but, if the king should prove
so bad as the world suspecteth or speaks of him,
Sebastian promised his sister to have in memory
what she advised him.   She answered, he should
do well to remember it, and to perform it.   " I
shall," saith he.   " I fear it," said she: At which
word pausing a while, leaning his head upon his
hand, he replied: " Sister, what will you say, if
the next news you hear of me shall be that I am
entered to be a monk in the Charter-house ? "   " A
monk !" she saith.   " I fear, rather, I shall see
thee hanged. (Not many years after she saw both.)
I pray God keep thee a good Christian; for such
perfection is fit for men of other metal than loose
Courtiers."   So smiling her brother took his
leave and returned to thc Court.

The king went forward in his luxurious designs,
advanced to dignities, and the greatest offices,
corrupt and dissolute persons, such as flattered
him in his unchaste and violent proceedings, abas-
ing and displacing the worthy and virtuous.
When Sebastian noted this with grief and trouble
of mind, perceiving the horrible mists and temp-
ests that these courses of the king did threaten

to the kingdom and reflecting upon the discourse
he had with his sister, he resolved to deliver himself from the snares of the Court, and the dangers of the world, and so as to betake himself in
time to a more secure harbour. Neither his
place in Court, nor the favour of the king, nor
his hopes of higher advancement did move him.
With a firm resolution he renounced all, and
entered Religion among the Carthusians in the
Charterhouse in London; a Religion, that in
England had especial veneration.

When his sister understood this she wondered
not a little that her brother should make so sudden a change, imagining it to be rather a delu-
sion, and temptation of the devil; first carrying
him to so high a pitch, and after to throw him
down. For this alteration on the sudden from
such delicateness, from such a place of ambition,
and liberty of conversation, to such austerity,
and despising of human glory, and recollection,
and strait silence, and perpetual clausure, bred
these fears in her mind. Albeit his inclination
was not of the worst, yet she held him no better
than others in the Court of honest name; never
dreaming of any such perfection, as that he
should enter an order so different from his bring-

ing up; for in his life, he could never digest fish,
but if eaten, he would vomit it up again; and
this order must never taste flesh.

Thus discussing with herself, she resolved to
ride to London, to see him, and inform the Prior
her opinion of it; so she took her journey, and
came to the Charterhouse. She there desired to
speak with the Father Prior, who coming to her,
after due salutation, he heard her discourse of her
brother. She advised the Prior to consider
well the admittance of him into his order. For
it seemed to her a thing unlikely, that one having
to that time passed his life in wordly content-
ments, should on the sudden be fit for so strait
and austere a religion. The Prior answered,
" Good Lady, thanks be to God, fit enough;"
and that she should not trouble herself with this
care. Her brother had passed his youthful years
and was now a judicious man; he had well considered what he took in hand, and had already
given sufficient proof, that the grace of God had
moved and drawn him to this estate, and His
Divine Providence had guided him to this order;
and that from having been a remarkable courtier,
he gave confidence to become a notable Carthusian. " If it be so," answered she, " blessed be

God, and blessed the day, in which he was born, that hath made so wise choice, so contrary to my opinion. I may then say, the happy lot is fallen upon him."

With that, the Prior commanded Brother Sebastian to be called; who being come before his sister, tears gave her not leave to speak. It was not so much the alteration of his person and habit which did move her, as his gesture, his retired speech, his grave humility and modesty astonished her; he so demeaning himself, as if he had been all his life in the monastery. With this she rested so content, as she could wish no more; for this she reported herself. Growing more tender with this unexpected joy, she took her leave of the Father Prior, and the novice-monk, her brother, commending to Almighty God his perseverance in that happy estate, and herself, and hers to their good prayers. Worthy Sebastian went so forward, and profited in his religion and studies, as he took holy Orders, and was made Priest.

The king blinded with his sensual humour, made a quarrel against the Apostolic See, that would not give allowance to his divorce. He attempted an utter breach, and disclaimed all obedience, rending himself and the kingdom from the unity of the Catholic Faith, and making it high treason to acknowledge obedience to the Apostolic See of Rome. Holiness of life now began to be suspected as dangerous; religion oppressed; good men evil entreated and afflicted; and all things in a manner without term of reason or justice in religious matters. When goodly and virtuous men perceived and felt this, and namely the Fathers of the Charterhouse; who began to bewail the evils and miseries of the times, (which never standing at a stay daily spread further); they therefore did shortly expect some sorrow to fall upon themselves in particular. For, when the king had published that profane and sacrilegious law,—commanding all to acknowledge and to swear that he was the Supreme Head of the Church within his Dominions, (a law that was never heard of before in any Christian Commonwealth) supposing, that it would seem harsh to wise and intelligent men, —he advised with his counsel; and resolved first to draw to his will such as were of note, for either their good life or learning. If these were

once gained, on whom the eyes of others were set,
others might the more easily be brought and
drawn to pretended submission.

Upon this device, having found by trial that
fair promises and sweet persuasions prevailed
nothing upon men constant in God's service, the
king determined by violence and cruelty to force
them to it. Whereupon, his wicked and sacrilegious ministers, set first upon the Fathers of
the Charter House of London, in which monastery at that time were two other priors of the
Carthusians, about business of the convents of
their order; namely, Father Robert Lawrence,
Prior of Beverly; and Father Augustine Webster,
Prior of Hexham; with the Prior of the same
house of London, Father John Haughton. All
of these were very grave men, known to be men
prudent, virtuous, and learned. With these three
they first began by propounding to them the
published edict of the King's Supremacy, to
swear and subscribe to it. The venerable fathers
answered : "This is a strange question to us,
and unheard of before;" for that they had not
read nor known the like example in the Church
of God ; which, in spiritual causes, is first to be
heard, being the Spouse of our Lord Jesus Christ,

guided and directed by His Holy Spirit; to which
the laws of men ought to be subordinate. Sir
Thomas Cromwell (who was Vicar General for
the king in spiritual matters, and chief com-
missioner in this business) replied, reviling them
with very base and scurril terms, calling them
Knaves and Traitors in refusing it; and pressing
them to swear entirely and distinctly to all that
was demanded, whether the Law of God permitted it, or not permitted it.   The Fathers
excused it, saying : "that they were priests and
sons of the Catholic Church, whose doctrine
they must follow and obey Her precepts."   The
impious Vicar answered, "I have nought to do
with your Church; if you will not submit yourselves to the king's law, I will persecute you, and
your order, nor will I leave until I have destroyed
you all."   But these good Fathers, choosing
rather to displease the king than God, were with
two other priests, carried to prison; where after
much vile entreaty, and divers examinations,
they were brought after five days to the bar, and
condemned to death.   On the 4th of May in the
year 1535, they were in their religious habits
drawn to Tyburn, there hanged, cut down while
they lived, and quartered, and their quarters were

set upon the gates of the City, and those of the
Prior of London, upon the gates of his own
monastery.

Three weeks following, on the 25th of May,
when these cruel ministers of justice saw that
this savage handling of the foresaid fathers
availed nothing to quail or lessen the courage
and constancy of the rest, they took other three
prisoners of the house of London, Father Sebastian Nudigate, Father Humphery Middlemore,
Vicar of the convent, and Father William
Exmew, Procurator, both of them learned in the
Greek and Latin tongues, and greatly respected
in their order. Although they were not very
aged in years, yet they were ancient and reverent
in their deportment and of a gravity and holy
conversation. These three fathers they drew
out of the cloister with inhuman violence, led
them to the Marshalsea, where they kept them
fourteen days bound to pillars, standing upright,
with iron rings about their necks, hands, and
feet. This cruel usage was caused to force them
to yield to the king's pleasure, and to subdue
them, if possible, to subscribe to the law of his
supremacy. When the king understood their
constancy, supposing he had some interest in

Father Sebastian, he went disguised to the prison
to speak with him. He called for him, gave him
to understand the care he had of him, seeing he
came in person to visit him, and to advise him
not wilfully to destroy himself, knowing the
danger of the law, and what others of his profession had suffered for their contempt and
disobedience. He added the many graces and
favours he had done him ; his ingratitude to be
of the number of those few, who, like traitors,
denied to conform themselves, as many others
both religious and all of the nobility had done ;
which obstinacy could not be excused. He told
him that he was like to suffer greater torments
if he did continue in his folly and would not
apply himself to what he demanded, being bound
to obey his Lord and King, and do what he
commanded ; "which, (saith the king) if thou
wilt do, thou shalt see that I have will to do thee
all favours, and power to accomplish them." A
mighty temptation and great encounter.

The good Father answered : "I must acknowledge this for a special and great honour,
yea far greater than my unworthiness can
deserve, that your Majesty hath vouchsafed, in
so undecent a lodging, to visit your poor servant,

and so poor a Religious. I confess I have
received many great favours of your Majesty.
God Almighty reward you, which I daily ask of
His Divine Majesty; and I shall, while I live,
pray for your health and prosperity, and for the
happiness of your kingdom. I am a Religious
man, and therefore more obliged sincerely to
speak the truth. The desire to save my soul,
which our Lord Jesus Christ redeemed with so
great cost as the price of His Life, and the
shedding of His most precious Blood, insinuating
and dictating to my soul the hazards and dangers
of the world, to retire myself from them (otherwise my demerits might suddenly have overthrown
me) to this port of Religion, wherein I daily
commend, as all of our order do, the welfare
and life of your Majesty to Almighty God, to
multiply His graces towards you, and prosper
you with all desired felicity; taking the same
our Lord Jesus Christ for witness, that it is
neither contempt, nor obstinacy, nor discontent,
nor intent of gainsaying, nor counsel of any that
hath power to withdraw my submission to the
law, or to make me not to yield to the oath
propounded, but the doctrine of the Holy Church
and the Law of God, the offence whereof I may

not incur." The king would have no more; but went away in a great rage threatening and cursing.

After fourteen days that these good fathers had suffered this cruel torture, they were brought before certain Lords of the Privy Council, examined apart, and again demanded concerning this new Law of Supremacy, which, they said, had banished all foreign authority. Their answer was, "that the authority of the Church was not foreign in any Christian country; and that in no sort could they yield to any thing not agreeable to the Law of God, or contrary to the doctrine of our holy Mother the Church."

After divers examinations, promises and threats, finding them still constant, and that they could not be brought to any consent in this matter, they were sent as prisoners to the Tower of London, where they remained some eight days. The king being there, set again upon Father Sebastian, not with mild speeches as before, but with menaces and injurious words. Notwithstanding, this undaunted Confessor hears him with patience, and answereth: "When in Court I served your Majesty, I did it loyally and faithfully; and so continue still your humble servant, although kept in this prison and bonds. But in matters that belong to the Faith and the glory of our Lord Jesus Christ, to the doctrine of the Catholic Church and the salvation of my poor soul, your Majesty must be pleased to excuse me." The King replies: "Art thou wiser and holier than all the Ecclesiastics and Seculars of my kingdom?" He answered: "I may not judge of others; nor do I esteem myself either wise or holy, being far short in either; only this I assure myself that the Faith and doctrine which I profess is no new thing, nor now invented, but always among the faithful, held for Christian and Catholic. We must obey God rather than man."

The king, having this resolute answer, would not use further discourse, but called him traitor; and, marvellously enraged, told him he should suffer for such a one. No device or battery could make any entrance into that valourous breast armed with the Spirit of God, resting immovable like a firm rock, remembering the Divine counsel of the Psalmist: "Put not your trust in princes nor in children of men, in whom there is no salvation:" and like to that immortal

Macchabee who did not fear to say even to the face of King Antiochus : " We will not obey the king's precept, but the law of the Lord which is given unto us."

On the 18th of June, these three fathers were brought to Westminster to be tried before the Judges ; where being indicted of high treason for refusing to subscribe and swear to the new-exacted oath of the King's Supremacy, they were again examined and demanded whether they would relent, and shew their obedience as other subjects did. They answered alike, that in that case, they neither could, nor would, nor ought to do it ; citing and alleging divers authorities of the Divine Scripture, of the ancient Fathers, and of the Sacred Canons ; proving and confirming that no temporal Prince can lawfully arrogate to himself the Church's government which the King of kings and Supreme Lord Christ Jesus gave and granted only to St. Peter and his Successors. They understanding and confessing this to be commanded by the Word of God, it were temerity and sin to go from this Faith, or to oppugn it. They were ready to have declared this with a grave and learned discourse if they had been permitted ; still showing a firm

resolution and valorous constancy in this doctrine.
The Judges seeing no remedy, proceeded against
them according to the form of their Laws, re-
mitting them to a Jury of twelve men, by whom
they were judged Guilty and convicted of high
treason. But before the Judge would pronounce
sentence of death, he used many reasons and
persuasions now at last to yield and conform
themselves; assuring them, upon submission,
of the king's mercy, and withall wishing them
to consider of the loss of so many good parts
which might be serviceable to God and beneficial
to their country. He spoke of the hastening of
their end with an infamous death; the grief of
their friends; the scandal of their kindred. In
particular he addressed himself to Father Sebastian, repeating to him the nobility of his blood,
the honourable allies he had in that kingdom,
the duty he owed to his Majesty having been
his servant; the many favours he had received
from him; which if they would consider and be
submissive, he did assure them there was place
for mercy and pardon. But no persuasions could
move minds so generous and so fixed in the love
of God; who desired nothing more than to die
for His cause, and to shed their blood for the

D

Catholic Faith. They made little reckoning
of these vain and worldly considerations, and
with great courage and constancy expected the
sentence, which then was given in this manner :
That they were found guilty of high treason,
were to return to the place from whence they
came and from thence to be drawn to the place
of execution, where they were to be hanged ; and
then presently to cut the halter ; their bowels
to be pulled out ; their bodies to be quartered
and the quarters to be set up where the Justice
should dispose them.

The Reverend good Fathers heard and received
this cruel sentence, answering with alacrity of
countenance " *Deo Gratias*," giving praise to our
Saviour Jesus Christ for this gracious favour to
make them worthy to suffer for His Faith and
the defence of His Church. So they were
returned to the prison : and the next day (the
19th of June) the sentence was executed. These
blessed Fathers were then taken out of the
prison, were laid stretched along bound upon
hurdles and so drawn with horses through the
streets of London to Tyburn, the place of execution. It was a lamentable spectacle to see
innocent Religious men in their venerable

habits, for profession of the ancient Catholic
Faith to be thus handled by such as professed
themselves Christians.

' Being arrived at the place of execution, they
praised Almighty God. They were patient to
perform what the officers commanded; willingly
and joyfully offering their bodies to that cruel
and inhuman death for the honour of the Faith
of Christ and the unity of His holy spouse the
Church. No reason (for many were used and
urged) availed to make any change in their minds
or wills to obey the king's law. They untied
Father Sebastian from the hurdle with the rope
about his neck, put him in the cart; there he
commended himself to the prayers of the good
assistants; prayed for the king that God Almighty
would give him long life and health, and His
grace to have care of his salvation and of the
good of his kingdom that had flourished so long
in Christian Religion, and in the unity and obedience of Christ's Catholic Church. He intimated
his own innocence both to the King and all the
world, and that his death was only for the
testimony and defence of the Catholic Faith, as
their judges could do no less than testify. And
so preparing himself to die said in Latin the

Psalm : "In Thee, O Lord, have I hoped, let me never be confounded," to the verse, "Into Thy Hands I commend my spirit: Thou hast redeemed me, O Lord, the God of truth." Then the cart being drawn away he remained hanging a very little or no space; for both he and the other two Fathers were cut down, being yet alive; presently bowelled; their bowels cast into the fire, their heads cut off, their bodies quartered and their quarters set up in the high ways and upon the gates of London. And in executing this barbarous cruelty upon such innocent persons, also was added this inhumanity, the second that was executed was made to stand to behold the death and the bloody slaughter of the first; and the third of them both, and this tyranny to see the bloody rending of their dear brethren.

This was the violent death but most happy end of Father Sebastian, an approved valorous gentleman, a perfect Religious, and a glorious Martyr of Christ Jesus. He was a singular honour of his house and an immortal renown of his family. For in nothing that doth illustrate the house of the Duchess (although descended from great Princes) is her blood more honoured than in this her kinsman and uncle, so illustrious and famous a martyr, so worthy a Religious, and so constant a servant of Christ Jesus; who in the first risings and oppositions against the Catholic Faith in our country so valiantly stood for it, and for the defence thereof sealed it with his blood and life.

This gentleman, as he has been described to me, was somewhat tall of stature, his body well proportioned and comely, his aspect lively and settled. He had great courage; his behaviour was pleasing, carrying it with a natural honesty and remarkable modesty. But after that he became a Religious, these parts of nature and education were much magnified by those of grace and piety, as hath been showed.

CHAPTER III.

THE elder sister of this glorious martyr was the
virtuous lady we now treat of, the grandmother
of the Duchess. Another sister was married to
Sir Leonard Chamberlain of Oxfordshire, mother
to the Lady Stonor, renowned for her zeal in
Catholic Religion, whom I saw, (being a boy), in
Oxford, convented there before the Judges for her
recusancy about the 23rd or 24th year of Queen
Elizabeth.[1] When she was reproved for her
constancy in the Catholic Religion, (which was
punishable by the laws of England,) she answered:
"I was born in such a time when Holy Mass
was in great reverence, and brought up in the
same Faith. In King Edward's time this
reverence was neglected and reproved by such as

---

[1] That is, about A.D. 1581 or 1582.

governed. In Queen Mary's, it was restored with much applause; and now in this time it pleaseth the state to question them, as now they do me, who continue in this Catholic profession. The state would have these several changes, which I have seen with mine eyes, good and laudable. Whether it can be so, I refer it to your Lordships' consideration. I hold me still to that wherein I was born and bred; and find nothing taught in it but great virtue and sanctity; and so by the grace of God I will live and die in it." This answer seemed to amaze the judges, spoken with great confidence; so they dismissed her upon ordinary sureties. This lady was generally noted for her rare devotion and marvellous abstinence, being widow even to her death.

Two other Sisters were Religious, one was Abbess of the Monastery of Sion by Brentford in Middlesex, who were of the holy order of St. Bridget, and yet continues entire in Lisbon and Portugal, brought out of England by the Lady Duchess when she came thence into Flanders; and there placed for some years until they removed to Spain. The other sister was of the order of St. Dominic. Both of them were exemplars for government and sanctimony of life. Two of their brothers were Knights of Rhodes, of the order and habit of St. John. In the year 1522 Rhodes was bravely besieged by Solyman, the great Turk, and valiantly defended by the Christian Knights of that Order, in which war both these brothers spent their lives.

The wisdom and virtue of Jane Dormer's grandmother were likewise well apparent in what she did, in marrying her son, Sir William. For when she saw the corruption of the state of this kingdom, and that those who by their authority and greatness should have been defenders of justice and religion, did seem to affect the contrary, her desire was to marry him with some virtuous gentlewoman answerable in quality. Sir Robert Dormer, her husband, liked it well, referring to her the charge of it, and wished her so to dispose it before the king should take notice of him, and hinder their intention by his command. For being their only child and heir to a great patrimony, many courtiers sought to him to marry their daughters with him, amongst whom Sir Francis Brien, a notorious favourite of the king; who much pretended to have him for husband to his niece, Jane Seymour. The power of this knight by

his privacy with the king was great, whom to
gainsay, there was more use of prudence than
will, when he seriously treated the business of
this marriage with Sir Robert Dormer, the father.
In the interim that this treaty was entertained
between them two, the mother, detesting the
conditions of this knight, took her son and rode
up to London to Sir William Sidney's house,
having before made an overture to the Lady
Sidney, who was well pleased. There the two
ladies made up the match between the son of
the one and the eldest daughter of the other.
Which when Sir Francis Brien understood,
seeing his pretence deluded was ill-pleased; but
the lady took the business and blame upon
herself, assuring him that she had treated the
matter before with the Lady Sidney and could
not go back. When he solicited the marriage
for his niece, he sent them word that they should
see his niece as well bestowed. For he, carrying
her up to the Court, placed her with the Lady
Anne Boleyn, the Queen, in whose service the
king affected her, for which there was often
much scratching and bye blows between the
queen and her maid. In the end queen Anne
Boleyn was imprisoned, condemned and beheaded

for foul adultery. The next day after, the king
married the Lady Jane Seymour, and had by
her the king his son. The Lady Dormer in
this prudent and valorous act shewing the
singular affection that she had to piety and
Christian Religion, and the respect she had
to chaste and honest conditions, to have her
son matched in a kindred of good fame, that
neither the power of so great a favourite nor
the gaining of so mighty a friend in Court, nor
the present possession of a great dowry, nor
the hopes of increase of honours, wealth and
advancement by his means, nor the fear of
inconveniences, that his displeasure might
procure, could move this lady to marry her son
with his niece who had made shipwreck of his
Faith and honesty.

After King Henry died, when the child King
Edward began to reign, the observance of
Catholic piety was put to flight and abolished, as
far as the public government could prevail, and
heresy and schism brought in place. In order
that it might take the deeper root, apostate
priests and friars from foreign parts, with all
their wives, were entertained in this kingdom,
and sent to be public Preachers in the Uni-

versities, and to teach heresies. If any pious or learned Catholic gainsaid (as many did) the doctrine of these outlandish apostates, they were persecuted, put to silence, deprived of their livings, imprisoned, or banished. This good lady, grandmother to the Duchess of Feria, whose house was a refuge to such persecuted men, gave them sustenance and security for their bodies; and received from them food and sustenance for the soul of herself, family, and neighbours. Notice hereof being taken by the Lady Mary, she did not a little favour her and hers, who, when she came to be Queen, this lady coming to her, she again remembered this hospitality, and very particularly thanked her for that charity, calling her the sustainer of the Catholic Faith. She, then commending to her Majesty divers of those good men, the Queen provided for all, entertaining some for her chaplains, and gave to others bishoprics, and other dignities. Such were the worthy persons to whom this good Lady gave hospitality.

If I should enter into particular discourse, what passed with this Lady in her charity and hospitality, it would contain many leaves of paper. For, wife and widow, being Lady of her house the space of three score years, it was her daily practice to give alms and to do pious works, as is confirmed by that which happened in this king's reign by the fame of her hospitality and charity. For, many disgusted with this strange change of Religion, and nothing yet established for the common service of God (so long were they hammering for five or six years a settled church-service and could not hit upon it, to the iking of all these heads) the people were also discontented with the political government. The great ones banded against each other and sought to destroy one another. Divers that had authority and command in their country, took advantage of the times and appropriated to themselves divers grounds, that were common, and useful to the public. Inferior gentlemen, who were rich and had more power than their neighbours, following the example of their great masters, took also into their particular possession some fields and pastures which had been common to the neighbourhood. The people in many places grieving and complaining of their wrongs, as they termed them, and hoping of no redress by authority, in sundry shires took the matter into their own hands to revenge themselves of these public

injuries; and seditiously growing together took
up arms, menacing and exclaiming against the
practisers of these evils. They made spoil and
havoc, wheresoever they came, pulling up hedges,
breaking down pales, filling up ditches, robbing
houses and committing other infinite disorders,
so that gentlemen were either forced to leave
their houses or with help of their neighbours so
to be guarded and strengthened as they might be
able to keep their houses and defend themselves
against the attempts of this fury.

To this Lady's house repaired many of all
sorts, from the villages round about, with their
wives and children, and the best moveables they
had; but all, with arms offering to defend her
person and to guard her house. The good Lady
welcomed them with many thanks, knowing that
in such furious tumults there is little regard or
respect to law or justice; and so fortified her
house with such strength and order as was convenient. Which when the rebels understood,
and the provisions she had made for her defence;
they sent her this message. That her Ladyship
should have no pain nor fear, for that her charity
and good works, known to the whole country,
were a sufficient guard and preservation of her

person and family, being renowned for her hospitality and christianity. They came not (as they
said) to spoil or do any hurt, but to restore to the
Commons that which was their own. Those
great fellows, who without justice, and those rich
ones, who without conscience, had appropriated
to themselves what belonged to the people in
common; these men were the marks they shot
at; and they should suffer the penance of their
cruelties and oppressions. And, as they promised, without doing any harm, more than going
through her grounds and treading the grass, they
marched forward, not doing nor offering the least
occasion of wrong or offence to any person or
goods belonging to her. Whereas in the parks
and lands of the gentlemen round about her they
made miserable spoil and committed many vio-
lences.

When it pleased God to take from this world
Sir Robert Dormer, her husband, having been
married about forty years, her son Sir William
Dormer had been married to a second wife, after
he had been widower nine years. He had by his
first wife (as hath been said) only two daughters,
and now had by this second a son, (who is now
the Lord Dormer) who was of the age of five

months when his grandfather died. This Lady
now a widow, being, disburdened of the obligations of a wife, did according to the counsel of
St. Paul, attend with more liberty to the service
of God. In both estates she showed herself an
imitable pattern for noble women to follow and
a mirror to behold. For, being married, she had
care, (as is shewed) to accomplish that which
appertained to the duty of a wife, by living
always in grateful love and due respect of her
husband; by governing her house in good order,
by directing her family with praiseable discretion,
by bringing up her son and grand-children (who
had lost their mother) in virtue; and in fine, she
behaved herself like a provident, wise and prudent lady and a careful good mother. In her
widow's estate, she retired herself somewhat
more from the encumbring of worldly affairs,
retaining some care yet, as one well experienced,
of her son's estate. She had her jointure and
living, severed from his, being sufficient and
answerable to the quality of the person, which
she well employed. She spent much time in
prayer and devotion, and never failed, (having
health,) at divine service. Her labours and

exercises were for the Church, and to do good to such as were in necessity.

It was not long after the death of Sir Robert Dormer, her husband, that King Edward died; to whom succeeded the Catholic Princess, Queen Mary, who obtained a renowned victory without fighting or shedding much blood against the Duke of Northumberland, who had set up his daughter-in-law, the Lady Jane Grey.[2] In this noise and tumult of war, to put down the right Queen and maintain the usurper, Sir William Dormer, this Lady's son, called friends and gathered strength to assist Queen Mary. Upon occasion, he went with them to Aylesbury, understanding that the Earl of Bedford would be there with his adherents for the county of Buckingham to proclaim the Lady Jane. Mr. Dormer encountering him there, told him plainly, " My Lord, we cannot hear of any Queen but the Lady Mary; and he that presumes publicly to name

---

[2] A proclamation of Jane Grey as Queen requiring the persons therein addressed to proceed in her behalf to suppress the advancement of Mary's supporters in Buckinghamshire, may be seen in Hare. M.S. 416. fol. 30. It is dated at the Tower of London, 18 July, in the first year of her reign. See the Chronicle of Queen Jane by J. G. Nichols, p. 109.

any other, shall do it to his cost." This so affrighted the Earl that he durst not attempt what was enjoined; and he retiring, Mr. Dormer went with his friends and followers to attend Queen Mary. This did he for his zeal to Right and Justice, not respecting alliance or kindred, for, his first wife, that was mother to the duchess, was cousin german removed to the Lady Jane. For this service and for the great charity of his mother to Catholic learned men in King Edward's days, (as hath been said) he was much favoured by the Queen, who appointed him one of the six Knights of the Bath in her coronation; she also had his daughter the Duchess in her [service, whom she much loved and esteemed, as hereafter shall be more particularly declared.

In this Queen's reign, which was a few months more than five years, this Lady remained with her son, continuing her piety among her neighbours. But when this virtuous and Catholic [Queen died, there died with her the upholding of piety and religion in England. For in the year 1558, Queen Elizabeth succeeding, altered the government, entertained heresies; the defenders] of them being her chief counsellors and commanders. This good Lady seeing this lament-

E

able alteration, although full of years, such was her zeal and love to the observance of true religion, as she left house, son, country, and friends; choosing rather a banished life to serve freely Almighty God than to remain in a kingdom so perverted and corrupted. With this Christian and zealous purpose in the year 1559, she passed the seas with her granddaughter, the Duchess of Feria, into Flanders. And a little before the Duchess parted from Mechlin for Spain, she went to Louvain, there to keep a house and settle herself; where resided many worthy and learned English priests, exiled for not conforming themselves to the new and heretical injunctions of England. There she lived the rest of her years (which were about twelve) with so great fame of virtue, piety, charity, and other Christian works, as not only that town and university but the country about did much reverence and honour her; and she is yet among the old people that knew her, remembered with renowned commendation. Yea, such were her works of liberality and piety as the learned Doctor Sanders in his book entitled " Visibilis monarchia Ecclesiæ,"[2] praiseth her as an eye-witness

---

[2] P. 708, ed. Lovan. 1571.

in these words: "The noble widow the Lady
Jane Dormer, grandmother of the most illustrious
Duchess of Feria, when she saw her country
overrun by heresy, willingly exiling herself, hath
so lived in Louvain for these twelve years as not
only she hath kept herself from all schism, but
also hath been a foot to the lame, an eye to the
blind, a staff to the weak, a true mother of
orphans, and a patroness of widows." Like
another Dorcas she made many coats and
garments for widows and poor people. When
the Duke of Alva was general in those countries,
his army was dispersed into divers towns, of
whom there was a garrison of many soldiers in
Louvain, who were pressed by necessity for want
of clothes and meat. This good lady had provided in her house, a chamber which was fraught
with cassocks, doublets, hose, stockings, hats
and shirts, for poor soldiers, of whom, at a time,
she had clothed forty soldiers and thirty soldiers.[8]
Which, when the duke understood, he gratefully
acknowledged the great obligations to her love
and charity by giving her extraordinary privileges
and exemptions for herself, house, and company.
He esteemed her in that degree, that when the

[8] So the original

magistrates of Louvain pretended any suit from
the duke, they took this readiest means and help
by her assisting commendations, naming her
their patroness and protectress.

Always in the Holy Week on Maunday
Thursday, this lady called together twelve
widows, or rather poor women, washed their
feet herself, gave every one a new gown, a smock,
a little purse with money, and her dinner that
day, and on Easter day following. Her house
was a refuge and harbour for banished priests
and Catholic gentlemen of her country; many
poor students were daily relieved by her, as of
this day some living, in my hearing have given
grateful testimony. People of all conditions
much respected her; the greatest of titles, lords
and ladies, often visited her, and had her in
especial regard. The university and town of
Louvain honoured her exceedingly, as the many
courtesies she received from them in life, and the
honour they did her after her death do well
testify.

In the year 1571, the 7th of July, this lady
(being about eighty years of age), left this natural
life to live for ever with God Almighty. After
having received with great devotion the holy

Sacraments of the Church, she remained to the last hour in good sense, and judgment, with great quietness and security of conscience. She had ordained her testament; bequeathed large alms to the poor, to colleges, to Religious, both men and women, of sundry monasteries; had left her lands and rents to her son as heir of them, and the goods that remained, absolutely to the disposing of the duchess, her grand-daughter, to whom her affection was ever most particular; for naming her or writing to her, still used this term: "My most dear and beloved daughter;" as appears in her will, the copy whereof I have. Her soul she commended to Him Who created and redeemed it; which, so full of good works no doubt and abounding with so many pious and Christian deeds of exemplar charity, ascended to Him without stay, as may morally be believed.

Her body when it was buried, was done with the solemnity fitting her quality. Many orphans, widows, and poor people according to her testament, were clothed, who attended the funeral. The prelates, doctors, regents, and chief of the university, the religious of all Orders, did go in their places. The gentlemen and magistrates of the town, accompanied likewise in their rank,

with the rest of the mourners to the church of
the Charter-house, where she was buried. And
the next day following, a great number of the
poor of the town (an example seldom seen, and
worthy the consideration) assembled together at
this lady's house; and every one, a candle lighted
in their hands, went in orderly procession, the
way that her body was carried the day before, to
the Charter-house, bewailing their loss, and
praying for her soul. Which action of their
memorable love came from their own motive and
gratitude.

She was buried, as I say, in the church of the
Charter-house (where she could not be admitted
in life by reason of her sex) in the middle of the
choir, just before the High Altar; where also
lieth buried with her, the body of the Lady Anne
Hungerford, her grand-daughter, only sister by
father and mother to the duchess, who thirty-two
years after died in the same town of Louvain,
and there both lie reconded under a fair marble
tomb, underset with marble pillars; their por-
traitures cut very lively in alabaster at length
lying upon the top. Epitaphs and escutcheons
of their descent and matches were erected at
the cost of the duchess, with an annual rent for

ever of a hundred florins given by her to the
same Charter-house paid out of the Town house
of Antwerp.

This Lady Hungerford, the year that her
grandmother died, came out of England, being
over the seas, before she understood of her death,
whose Catholic piety and noble desires could not
content her husband, Sir Walter Hungerford ;
who albeit nobly descended, yet by base covet-
ousness and disordered sensual living much
blemished his person and worth.   He did not
entreat his lady as was due to his wife and a
gentlewoman of her rank, whereupon she pretended his leave to go beyond seas to her
grandmother, where she might have liberty of
conscience and serve God freely.   In this he,
to have more liberty for his sensual appetites,
and to avoid the troubles for her conscience, nct
unwillingly consented ; and so, as I say, she
passed to the Low Countries where she lived
thirty-two years, with great example of true
nobility and Christianity, much honoured for her
rare parts of valour, and discretion, the memory
whereof remains in Namur and Louvain, in
which places she for the most part lived.
Madam Margaret of Austria, Duchess of Parma,

sister to King Philip II. of Spain, then Governess
of these provinces for her brother, took much
contentment in her conversation, knowing her to
be the duchess' sister, honoured her with very
special affection, invited her often, commending
to divers her noble behaviour and the worth of her
parts such as she knew in very few women; as
the party who heard her highness speak it, told
me. The governors and magistrates of the
towns where she lived in all imminent dangers
(for then the war in those parts was hot) took
particular regard to her, came to her house, presented all the security they could for her person,
goods, and family; thereby assuring the great
care they had of her safety. Such was the merit
of her carriage. And when fears or dangers
occurred, her courage and magnanimity were
rare and generous. To gentlemen distressed and
poor students, her liberality was marvellous,
always compassionate, a great alms-giver. In
this her exile she had the grief to lose her only
son in the flower of his youth, in the state to
marry, a gentleman of great hopes, very noble in
condition, discreet and virtuous. A chastisement
which Almighty God lays upon adulterers, from
which crime, I wish his father had been innocent:

so his house might have continued in his blood, which now is dispersed.

This Lady Hungerford passed out of this world on the 19th of December, 1603, full of good works, imitating the steps of her worthy grandmother.[4]

In testimony of the worth and great merits these two ladies, not only the ordinary but the public voices of the country proclaim it, and such as served them many years; but the writings and assertions of the principal and most learned of our nation, then beyond the seas, do avouch the same; as for example that grave and learned Prelate, Dr. William Allen, afterwards Cardinal, Dr. Owen Lewis, Bishop of Cassano, Dr. Nicholas Sanders, Dr. Thomas Stapleton, both great writers and public readers of Divinity and others, to the number of fifty, who were petitioners to Pope Gregory the XIII., to procure the duchess to be sent to the Low Countries. They, when treating the business with Cardinal Morono, their patron in the Court of Rome, and Protector of the English nation,

---

[4] The MS. here gives ten lines of Latin poetry, being a copy of the verses engraven "at the fore-end of her tomb."

among other reasons that they allege in a common letter, dated 28th December 1572, mention divers [5] favours, received from the duchess.

CHAPTER IV.

OF THE YOUTH AND EDUCATION OF JANE DORMER.

JANE DORMER, brought up under so worthy a matron, in her infancy, beginning to be of understanding, the first thing she learned was her duty to serve God, and her obedience to her father, grandfather, and grandmother, by conforming herself with affectionate humility to their commands. This virtue she so embraced, as with rare respect it continued with her, even to the death of her grandmother, although exalted to a higher rank. And when she served Queen Mary, being of her bedchamber, she never neglected her duty and obedience to her grandmother, never would do any matter of moment, without making her acquainted, and asking her

---

[5] "Dr. Sanders was the bearer of this letter." MS.

leave; and what she was commanded or advised by her, that did she carefully obey.

Before seven years she began to read the Primer, or as we call it, the Office of our Blessed Lady, in Latin; and from that time, daily continued it, having any possibility of health to the end of her life, which was sixty-seven years. In such curious works of the needle as gentlewomen learn, she attained a marvellous skill and perfection. For I have seen samplers, and divers of her works, wrought with her own hands, very curious, rare, and excellent, so adjudged by such as were held great mistresses in such works. Also divers dressings for the altar, and ornaments for the priests and such as serve at the altar, very rich and sumptuous, of notable invention and variety, all wrought by herself. Together with these abilities, she always retained a commendable modesty in all she did or spake.

Her grandfather Sir William Sidney, whom the king, though still carried away by his own exorbitant passions, did choose to be tutor and governor of his son Prince Edward, when remaining for a time at Ashridge, (which was not far from her grandfather Dormer's) sent for her to entertain some time with the prince. They

were both near of one age, about six or seven
years, the prince being only elder by three
months; he desired her company, taking particular pleasure in her conversation. Thither she
was sent with her governess, passing her time
with the prince, either in reading, playing, or
dancing, and such like pastimes, answerable to
their spirits and innocency of years, and in
playing at cards, would use this speech, as it
fell out: "Now Jane, your king is gone, I shall
be good enough for you."

I have heard them that were about the prince
avouch it, that his inclination and natural disposition was of great towardness to all virtuous
parts and princely qualities; a marvellous sweet
child, of very mild and generous condition.
Afterwards, when his father died, (he being but
nine years of age), mischievous and heretical
governors, contrary to his father's will, abused
his tender age; who ruling to effect their own
ends notoriously injured the natural good inclination of this gentle and noble prince. For,
when he was king, in passing by the ruins of
goodly monasteries, he demanded what buildings
were those? It was answered: That they were
religious houses, dissolved and demolished by

order of the king his father, for abuses. He
replied : "Could not my father punish the
offenders, and suffer so goodly buildings to stand,
being so great an ornament to this kingdom;
and put in better men, that might have governed
and inhabited them?" seeming to lament that
lamentable course. And when the Lady Mary,
his sister, (who ever kept her house in very
Catholic manner, and order) came to visit him,
he took special content in her company (I have
heard it from an eye-witness) he would ask her
many questions, promise her secrecy, carrying
her that respect and reverence, as if she had
been his mother. And she again in her discretion,
advised him in some things that concerned himself, and in other things that touched herself; in
all shewing great affection and sisterly care of
him. The young king would burst forth in tears,
grieving matters could not be according to her
will and desire. And when the duke his uncle
did use her with straightness and want of liberty;
he besought her to have patience until he had
more years, and then he would remedy all.
When she was to take leave, he seemed to part
from her with sorrow; he kissed her, he called
for some jewel to present her, he complained that

they gave him no better to give her. Which noted by his tutors, order was taken, that these visits should be very rare, alleging that they made the king sad and melancholy; and consulted to have afflicted her officers and servants; for that contrary to the then made law, she had public Mass in her chapel, if they could draw any assent from the king. But he, upon no reasons, would ever give way to it, and commanded strictly that she might have full liberty of what she would. He sent to her, inquiring if they gave her any trouble or molestation, for if they did, it was against his will, and he would see her contented. But it was not safe, nor did it stand with prudence, as the times went, for the Lady Mary to complain.

When Jane Dormer grew older, she was commended by her grandmother to the most noble and Catholic princess the Lady Mary, so persuaded by her grandfather Sidney, whom two of his daughters had served before and died in her service, much favoured by her Highness for their virtue. When the queens (the wives of King Henry) had sought with much importunity to have them in their service they would by no means leave the Lady Mary although the king

himself requested it.[1]   In those days the house
of this princess was the only harbour for honourable young gentlewomen, given any way to piety
and devotion.   It was the true school of virtuous
demeanour, befitting the education that ought to
be in noble damsels.   And the greatest lords in
the kingdom were suitors to her to receive their
daughters in her service.

   With the Lady Mary, Jane remained after the
time, when by the death of King Edward the
kingdom fell to her, and even till her decease out
of this world.   And being in her service was
particularly favoured by her and affected; with
which she corresponded with all dutiful respect,
so as seldom or never would the queen permit
her absence.   She slept in her bedchamber, many
times with her; she read together with her our
Lady's Office; she committed to her charge and
trust her usual wearing jewels and what else was
of esteem to be commended to one of her bed-
chamber.   At table, she eat the meat that the
hand of Jane Dormer carved for her, which is an
evident argument and proof of her virtues when

---

[1] Ladies of the name of Mabel and Elisabeth Sydney are
mentioned in Queen Mary's Household Book, pp. 119, 126, 184.

so virtuous a princess, and of so admirable parts did so much favour and esteem her.

This queen seldom went in progress except it were to the Cardinal's house at Croydon (for Cardinal Pole her kinsman was Archbishop of Canterbury) avoiding by all means to trouble and grieve her subjects in time of hay and corn harvest, when they had use of their horses and carts. And being at Croydon, for her recreation, with two or three of her ladies, she would visit the poor neighbours, they all seeming to be the maids of the Court; for then she would have no difference, and ever one of these was Jane. She would sit down very familiarly in their poor houses, talk with the man and the wife, ask them of their manner of living, how they passed, if the officers of the Court did deal with them, as such whose carts and labours were pressed for the queen's carriages and provisions.[2] And among others, being once in a collier's house, the queen sitting by while he did eat his supper, on her demanding the like of him, he answered, that they had pressed his cart from London, and had

---

[2] Various illustrations of Queen Mary's kindness and liberality towards the poor may be seen in her Privy Purse Expenses printed by Sir F. Madden. See p. 258.

not paid him. The queen asked if he had called for his money. He said, yea, to them that set him awork, but they gave him neither his money nor good answer. She demanded; "Friend," is this true, that you tell me?" He said, "Yea," and prayed her to be a mean to the comptroller, that he and other poor men might be paid. The queen told him she would, and willed that the next morning about nine or ten o'clock, he should come for his money. She came no sooner to the Court, but she called the comptroller,[8] and gave him such a reproof for not satisfying poor men, as the ladies who were with her, when they heard it, much grieved. The queen said that he had ill officers who gave neither money nor good words to poor men, and that hereafter he should see it amended, for if she understood it again, he should hear it to his displeasure; and that the next morning the poor men would come for their money, and that they should be paid every penny. Mr. Comptroller wondered how this came to the queen, and the ladies told him what had passed that evening.

[8] Probably Sir Robert Rochester, who was appointed by the Queen at her accession and continued in office till his death in December, 1557, or Sir William Kingston, who died in 1541.

In the visiting of these poor neighbours, if she found them charged with children, she gave them good alms, comforted them, advising them to live thriftily and in the fear of God, and with that care to bring up their children; and if there were many children she took order they should be provided for, placing both boys and girls to be apprentices in London, where they might learn some honest trade, and be able to get their living. This did she in a poor carpenter's house, and the house of the widow of a husbandman. And in this sort did she pass some hours with the poor neighbours, with much plainness and affability; they supposing them all to be the queen's maids, for there seemed no differnce. And if any complaints were made she commended the remembrance very particularly to Jane Dormer.

CHAPTER V.

THE MARRIAGE OF JANE DORMER WITH THE DUKE OF FERIA. SKETCH OF THE LIFE AND CHARACTER OF QUEEN MARY.

THESE special favours that the queen shewed to Jane Dormer, together with the rare parts of her mind and person, were occasion that divers of the greatest worth and nobility did seek her for marriage; as Edward Courtenay, Earl of Devonshire, son of the Marques of Exeter, and cousin-german removed of the queen, whom the queen delivered from the Tower at her entrance there, at the same time with the other prisoners, the Duke of Norfolk, and the Bishops Bonner, Tunstall, and Gardner. This last bishop would have made the match, finding the Earl to have an affection to her; and some were of opinion he did it to prevent his marriage with the Lady Elizabeth, whereof afterwards grew the greatest part of her troubles in Queen Mary's time. He

did solicit the queen about the match, and dealt
with the young lady, to have it effected. Also
the Duke of Norfolk was a suitor to her, being
at that time the only duke in England, and some
others of great quality, which the Duke of Feria
afterwards confesseth in his last will, making a
petition for her to the king, tells him that she
had refused greater matches than himself in her
own country. The Earl of Nottingham that now
is Lord Admiral, being of her years, and in that
time calling her mistress, told me, when he was
ambassador in Spain, in 1605, that she was the
fairest and the sweetest woman of the world;
and that the whole Court did admire her, and
bear her a reverent respect, as well for her own
worth, as for the esteem the queen did bear her.
But Jane in these pretences would do nothing,
without the consent of her Majesty, who had no
great will to leave her, and would say in the
treating of these matters, that Jane Dormer
deserved a very good husband; and would add
further, that she knew not the man that was
worthy of her. When it chanced that Jane was
not well, as that she could not well attend upon
the queen, it is strange the care and regard her
Majesty had of her, more like a mother or sister

than her queen and mistress. As in the last days of this blessed queen, she being at Hampton Court, and to remove to London, Jane having some indisposition, her Majesty would not suffer her to go in the barge by water, but sent her by land in her own litter, and her Physician to attend her. And being come to London, the first that she asked for was Jane Dormer, who met her at the stairfoot, told her that she was reasonably well. The queen answered "So am not I," being about the end of August, 1558. So took her chamber, and never came abroad again.

At that time the king was in Flanders about his wars, made upon the frontiers of France, who understanding the Queen's sickness, being then with his army before Dourlens,[1] sent away the Duke of Feria, to serve and assist her in all that should be requisite. It pleased Almighty God, that this sickness was her last, increasing daily, until it brought her to a better life. Jane was continually about the Queen, not yet married, for the Queen would not have her marry, until the king was returned from Flanders ; which occasioned the want of great gifts and rich endowments wherewith the Queen had determined and

[1] A fortified town, about eighteen miles north of Amiens.

promised to honour the marriage, whereof did
her Majesty complain. She finding herself lan-
guishing to death, told Jane, she would have been
glad to have seen her marriage had been effected
in her days ; but God Almighty would otherwise
dispose, and being sick and the king absent, she
was not in case to do what she would. Her sickness was such as made the whole realm to
mourn, yet passed by her with most Christian patience. She comforted those of them that grieved
about her ; she told them what good dreams she
had, seeing many little children like Angels play
before her, singing pleasing notes, giving her
more than earthly comfort ; and thus persuaded
all, ever to have the holy fear of God before their
eyes, which would free them from all evil, and be
a curb to all temptations. She asked them to
think that whatsoever came to them was by God's
permission ; and ever to have confidence that He
would in mercy turn all to the best.

From the time of her Mother's troubles, this
queen had daily use of patience and few days of
content, but only those that she established and
restored the Catholic Religion to her kingdoms.
While she was queen, in those few years, she
suffered many conspiracies, and all out of mali-

cious humours to God's truth. She gave commandment to all, both of her Council, and servants, to stand fast in the Catholic religion ; and
with those virtuous and Christian advices, still in
prayer and hearing good lessons, receiving the
holy Sacraments of the Church, left this world,
which was the 17th day of November, 1558. That
morning hearing Mass, which was celebrated in
her chamber, she being at the last point (for no
day passed in her life that she heard not Mass)
and although sick to death, she heard it with so
good attention, zeal, and devotion, as she answered in every part with him that served the
Priest ; such yet was the quickness of her senses
and memory. And when the Priest came to that
part to say, *Agnus Dei, qui tollis peccata mundi,* she
answered plainly and distinctly to every one,
Miserere nobis, Miserere nobis, Dona nobis pacem.
Afterwards seeming to meditate something with
herself, when the Priest took the Sacred Host to
consume it, she adored it with her voice and
countenance, presently closed her eyes and rendered her blessed soul to God. This the duchess
hath related to me, the tears pouring from her
eyes, that the last thing which the queen saw in
this world was her Saviour and Redeemer in the

sacramental species; no doubt to behold Him presently after in His glorious Body in heaven. A blessed and glorious passage. *Anima mea cum anima ejus.*

This good queen had commended in private divers things to Jane Dormer to give to the Lady Elizabeth her sister, and to tell her who was to succeed her in the kingdom; which she performed with dutiful fidelity, giving her the rich and precious jewels, that were in her custody,[2] which Queen Elizabeth willingly received, and sent her messages. These were to uphold and continue Catholic Religion, to be good to her servants, and to pay what might justly be required. But this of religion, I know not what reasons of base moment, or other circumstances of devilish policy had diverted her herein; notwithstanding before in the queen's sickness, she had faithfully promised the continuance; and all the reign of Queen Mary, the Lady Elizabeth did hear daily two masses, one for the living, another for the dead, seeming extraordinary devout to our Blessed Lady; and in her troubles being examined about religion, she prayed God, that the earth might

[2] The delivery of the jewels is the subject of two memoranda in the Record Office, Domest. Eliz. VIII. 24.

open and swallow her up alive, if she were not a
Roman Catholic.   And this is likewise confirmed
by the duke of Feria his letter to the king, who
in this sickness of the queen visited the Lady
Elizabeth, certifying him, that she did profess
Catholic Religion, and believed the Real Presence, and was not like to make any alteration
for the principal points of religion.

I will now speak somewhat of these two
queens' births.   And then of other passages of
their lives, whereof only the truth shall be
written, and most out of the testimonies of
protestant writers.

Queen Catharine was some five years older
than the king, and very different in manners.
She rose at mid-night to be present at the matins
of the Religious.   At five o'clock she made herself ready with what haste she might, saying
that the time was lost which was spent in ap-
parelling herself.   Under her royal attire she did
wear the habit of St. Francis, having taken the
profession of his Third Order.   She fasted all
Fridays and Saturdays and all the Eves of our
Blessed Lady with bread and water.   On Sundays she received the Blessed Sacrament, read
daily the Office of the Blessed Virgin, she was

the most part of the morning in the Church at
holy service and after dinner read the life of that
day's Saint to her maids standing by.   Then she
returned to the Church.   She was sparing in her
supper.   She prayed kneeling on her knees without cushions.   She was affable in conversation,
courteous to all, and of an excellent and pious
disposition.   This lady, a mirror of goodness,
was afterwards brought into infinite troubles, so
to be tried as that the sweet savour of her virtues
might be diffused over the whole christian world.

Henry the Eighth, weary (as it seems) of this
good queen Catharine, after fifteen years' co-habi-
tation, by the suggestion of Cardinal Wolsey begins
to make scruple whether this marriage with the
Lady Catharine was lawful, for that she had been
before his brother's wife.   Pope Julian the second
gave lawful dispensation to make good the
marriage.   That learned and glorious martyr
doctor John Fisher, the light not only of the
kingdom of England but of the whole Christian
world, when this divorce was in pleading, delivered to the legates a paper most learnedly written
in defence of the marriage, advising them not to
seek a knot in a rush nor to suffer the manifest
truth of Holy Scripture and Ecclesiastical laws

sufficiently seen and examined in this cause, to
be perverted; but rather to consider again and
again how great mischiefs would follow by this .
divorce, to wit, hatred between King Henry and
Charles the Emperor, and the factions of the
princes who would join them. And the most
grievous of all,—dissensions in matters of faith,
schisms, heretics and infinite sects. "I (said he)
have in this matter laboured much and employed
my utmost industry; and I dare affirm what I have
not only proved in this writing, and clearly taught
by the testimony of the Sacred Scriptures and of
Holy Fathers, but also am ready to testify it
with the shedding of my blood, that there is no
power on earth that can dissolve or disjoin this
marriage, which has been joined by God Himself."

This with other learned and pious writings
that the other advocates did present to the
legates, although Cardinal Wolsey was one, did
move them not to give sentence as the king
desired and required; nor would Clement VII.,
then Pope, give way to it, who then being at war
with the emperor was offered by King Henry to
maintain four thousand [men] in his wars
against Cesar. So much did he desire this

divorce to marry the Lady Anne Bullen. He
sought all means by gifts and corruptions to most
Universities to have their favourable opinions for
this his desire. Cardinal Wolsey had it intimated, in regard to his note to the emperor, that the
king might marry with the Lady Margaret, a
very fair woman, the widow of the Duke of
Alençon and sister to Francis, the French king.

Thomas Cranmer, chaplain to Sir Thomas
Bullen, the supposed father of the Lady Anne,
was a man to the king's own heart. He turned
as the king pleased, flattered and followed him
in all his demands. He pronounced the sentence
of divorce by which Queen Catharine was to be
called the princess dowager of Prince Arthur and
Anne was to be held lawful queen.

Mr. Camden conceals the time of the marriage
of Anne Bullen, for that the Lady Elizabeth's
birth was in four months after. I marvel that
he tells not the time of the king's espousals with
her, nor of her marriage and her coronation, she
being the mother of her whose life and reign he
published. He says only that she was born
7th September, 1533, at Greenwich. Queen
Catharine was banished from the Court to
Kimbolton, where living retired with her maids

until 6th January, 1536, she left this mortal life.
It is said that her days were shortened by the
intemperature of the unwholesome air, but
chiefly by the continual increase of griefs and
calamities; and some were of opinion, not without suspicion of poison, for the Lady Anne hated
her extremely. When the king understood her
death he shed tears and commanded all his
household to wear mourning; but his new wife
did clothe herself in yellow, glad of her death
that she died so quietly. Her body was buried
at Peterborough. She never could be persuaded
after her banishment from the Court to enter
into a monastery, although most desirous of that
life, nor to do anything that might be in prejudice
of her marriage, although exposed to many
injuries and manifest dangers. Nor could she be
drawn to go into Spain, or into Flanders, whither
she was invited by the emperor, her nephew,
where she might have had most honourable
entertainment. She applied these miseries and
disasters to have specially happened for the death
of Prince Edward Plantagenet, son of the Duke
of Clarence, brother to King Edward the Fourth;
whom (most innocent) Henry VII. put to death
to make the kingdom more secure to his pos-.

terity, and to induce King Ferdinand to give his daughter, this Catharine, in marriage to Prince Arthur. Before her death she wrote two pious letters, one to the king, the other to Friar Foster, her ghostly father, then in prison, after with cruel tortures a glorious martyr. Thus ended this great queen and holy princess, renowned in all nations and magnified by most writers of those times.

Within five months after, Queen Anne was brought to her reckoning for another world, but after a different life to her predecessor. It was passed most in masks, dancing, plays and such corporal delights, in which she had a special grace,—temptations to carnal pleasures and inventions to disgrace such and ruin them who were renowned for virtue. From the time that Queen Catharine was defended so stoutly and learnedly by the Bishop of Rochester she did seek by all means his destruction. One Richard Rice, a cook, was suborned to poison him, and he knew no other way to do it than to poison the common pot, which was for the whole household of the bishop. It chanced that that day according to his custom the bishop came not to dine in the parlour, but most of his family that dined there were poisoned and died thereof. Rice the cook being discovered did confess it and was publicly put to death for it. And when a gentleman brought word to the king that Sir Thomas More was then beheaded, the king being at table, and the Lady Anne standing by, the king throwing away the dice showed anger and sorrow that he was troubled and said to her, " This is long of you; the honestest man of my kingdom is dead," and suddenly retired chafing.

But to come to her death. The king seeming to affect Jane Seymour, and having her on his knee, as Queen Anne espied, who then was thought to be with child, she for anger and disdain miscarried, as she said, betwitting the king with it, who willed her to pardon him, and he would not displease her in that kind thereafter. But the queen, much wanting to have a manchild to succeed, and finding the king not to content her, to have her purpose did accompany with her own brother, Lord George Bullen, Viscount Rochfort, Francis Weston, Henry Norris, William Brereton and Mark Sweton, a musician, all of the Privy Chamber, for which they all suffered death. Three days after that Anne Bullen herself was beheaded on 14th May,

1536, the Duke of Norfolk sitting High Steward. She was convicted and condemned by twenty-six peers, whereof her father was one, who shortly after died of grief. She was not twenty-nine years of age. We see how different were the mothers of these two queens, and of the latter the father might be doubted, for Queen Mary would never call her sister, nor be persuaded she was her father's daughter. She would say she had the face and countenance of Mark Sweton, who was a very handsome man. But we will pass to their education.

To speak briefly of the education and some passages of the life of Queen Mary, I should relate that she was bred under her virtuous mother, as well in princely splendour, as in true piety, to know and serve Almighty God and to have His holy fear before her eyes; and afterwards was commended for her further education to the Countess of Salisbury, the mother of Cardinal Pole, and cousin german to the queen her grandmother, a most pious and saint-like woman. She was declared Princess of Wales and heir of the kingdom ; so bred as she hated evil ; knew no foul or unclean speeches, which when her lord father understood, he would not believe it but

would try it once by Sir Francis Brian, being at
a mask in the court ; and finding it to be true,
notwithstanding, perceiving her to be prudent and
of a princely spirit, did ever after more honour
her. It chanced once that she and the Lady
Anne Boleyn at Eltham, heard Mass together in
one room. At the end of Mass, the Lady Mary
made a low courtesy and went to her lodging; so
did the Lady Anne, then called queen. When
she came to her quarter, one of her maids told
her that the Lady Mary at parting made reverence
to her, she answered that she did not observe it ;
and said, "If we had seen it, we would have
done as much to her;" and presently sent a lady
of honour to her, to excuse it ; adding, that the
love of none should be dearer nor more respected
than hers, and she would embrace it with the
kindness of a true friend. The lady that carried
the message came when the Lady Mary was sat
down at dinner. When admitted, she said;
"The queen salutes your grace with much
affection and craves pardon, understanding that
at your parting from the oratory, you made a
courtesy to her, which if she had seen, she would
have answered you with the like ; and she desires
that this may be an entrance of friendly corres-

pondence, which your grace shall find completely
to be embraced on her part." "It is not possible," answered the Lady Mary, "that the queen
can send me such a message; nor is it fit she
should, nor can it be so sudden, her majesty
being so far from this place. You would have
said, the Lady Anne Boleyn, for I can acknowledge no other queen but my mother, nor esteem
them my friends who are not hers. And for the
reverence that I made, it was to the altar, to
her Maker and mine; and so they are deceived,
and deceive her who tell her otherwise." The
Lady Anne was maddened with this answer, replying, that one day, she would pull down this
high spirit.

Ludovicus Vives[1] dedicated to her in the year
1524, two hundred and thirteen *Symbola,* or short
and intricate sentences, in few words, which we
call commonly Mottoes, with paraphrasing upon
every one of them. The first was, *Scopus vitæ
Christus*; the last was, *Mente Deo defixus.* These
she seemed to have in perpetual memory, by the
practice of her whole life; for she made Christ
the beginning and end of all her actions, from
Whose goodness all things do proceed, and to

[1] In his Epistle to the Lady Mary, from Bruges, 1st July, 1524.

Whom all things do tend, having a most lively example in her virtuous mother.

All the neighbour-kings and princes did greatly desire her for marriage. James the Fifth, King of Scots, after, Charles the Emperor, offering presently to give the possession of the whole Low-Countries; then the French king for both his sons, first for the Dauphin, then for the Duke of Orleans; whom when King Henry did not accept, for their tender age, King Francis offered himself to marry her; such was the fame of her virtue and worth, in which for particular reasons of state, none of them succeeded.

In King Edward's reign, when new Governors altered the religion, she could nor would not be persuaded by any entreaties or threats of the Protector, or any others, to shut her oratory or keep close her chapel, which she had in her house, but openly to have Mass daily said, or suffer the least change in Catholic Religion. And when she saw the courses those new rulers took, in breaking her father's will, to which they were sworn before his death, she very courageously and roundly wrote to the Protector, admonishing him and the rest of the Council to look well what they did, not to abuse the king's minority in altering the laws,

will, and ordinances of his and her father King
Henry; for in doing so they might be called to
account about the same when the king her brother
should come to full years. And withal she told
them plainly, that they had no authority to make
such alteration in so great matters as they did ;
but rather to conserve things in the state left
unto them by the king her father, according to
the solemn oath they had sworn unto him before
his death, that they would do so, especially about
matters of Religion, until the king her brother
came to lawful age. And when they did not dare
publicly to persecute her, being the next to the
crown, they took from her her chaplains, punished them for not obeying the laws enacted ; whereof she complained to her brother and wrote to
the Emperor how they dealt with her chaplains
and servants. Which the Emperor took hardly
that that could not be permitted to her, which
was to all ambassadors of foreign Princes ; being
their king's elder sister, and professing the Catholic Religion in which she was bred and no other
known before those days in the kingdom of
England.

CHAPTER VI.

SKETCH OF THE REIGN OF QUEEN ELIZABETH. CONTRAST BETWEEN HER AND QUEEN MARY.

I NOW pass to the education of Queen Elizabeth. This would not be under her mother, for she was not three years of age when her mother died. She had been sworn princess of Wales a little after her birth, and the Lady Mary deprived. The king, shortly after her mother's death, in the beginning of the month of June called an assembly of the Bishops and a parliament, signifying how much it did displease and repent him of the wrong done his daughter Mary and the advancing of Elizabeth, Anne Boleyn's daughter; and would have it again as it was, and to constitute some certain faith and form of religion. For when Anne reigned all things were in confusion, a licentious liberty was among all, nor was it determined what they should believe or do in matters of religion. For she (miserable woman) was the first cause of the schism and bane of her

country. Yet she was a princess of majesty
and magnificence, and as one truly saith, fitter
for greatness than devotion and of more policy
than religion. Her sister Mary was no way
inferior as far as was fit for so great a princess,
only she was seventeen years older, but bred up
in all good learning, especially in virtue and
religion. Mr. Camden tells us that the Lady
Elizabeth read Melanchthon's Common Places; I
would she had in place thereof read St. Augustine's Meditations, Confessions and Soliloquies;
and for lives and living in matters of policy the
Saint's books *De Civitate Dei*.

A great lady, who knew her very well, being a
girl of twelve or thirteen, told me that she was
proud and disdainful, and related to me some
particulars of her scornful behaviour, which
much blemished the handsomeness and beauty
of her person. In King Edward's time what
passed between the Lord Admiral, Sir Thomas
Seymour, and her Dr. Latimer preached in a
sermon, and was a chief cause that the Parliament condemned tne Admiral. There was a bruit
of a child born and miserably destroyed, but
could not be discovered whose it was; only the
report of the midwife, who was brought from her

house blindfold thither, and so returned, saw
nothing in the house while she was there, but
candle light; only she said, it was the child of a
very fair young lady. There was a muttering of
the Admiral and this lady, who was then between
fifteen and sixteen years of age. If it were so, it
was the judgment of God upon the Admiral; and
upon her, to make her ever after incapable of
children. But the Admiral in September before
had buried his wife, Queen Catharine, who died
in childbed of a daughter. And it seems the cuck-
old then made no great reckoning of the Lady
Elizabeth, for the great Lord Master was in 1550
created earl of Wiltshire, which was the title and
honour of her father, transporting it from her and
from his blood. And when after the death of King
Edward they set up the Lady Jane they rejected
her, fearing only Queen Mary. The reason why
I write this is to answer the voice of my countrymen in so strangely exalting the Lady Elizabeth,
and so basely depressing Queen Mary.

Queen Elizabeth's troubles began in the second
year of her sister's reign. She was suspected and
accused to be assistant unto the rebellion of Sir
Thomas Wyatt, for which she was first committed to the Tower of London and afterwards re-

moved prisoner to Woodstock. Most of the
Council by the accusation of the delinquents and
other prescriptions would persuade the queen to
proceed against her by law; but her goodness
deferred it.

When Philip was come into England and
admitted king, finding the Lady Elizabeth to be
thus restrained, he dealt with the queen to be
merciful to her, and so delivered her not only
from extreme punishment but procured her
liberty to return to the Court. The remainder of
her sister's reign she lived for the most part in
her own house at Hatfield; to which place when
many suspected heretics and turbulent people
repaired, it seemed fit to the Privy Council that
the business should be no longer dissembled, but
questioned and punished. But the king and the
Spanish nobility favouring her, persuaded to
defer the matter. It broke out more manifest
the next year in March, when Sir Anthony
Kingston, Richard Udall, John Throckmorton,
John Daniel, William Stanton and others conspired together, not without counsel of the
French ambassador, to rob the king's treasure
which was provided for the French war. When
the matter was discovered by one of the con-

spirators, some were taken and executed, others
fled into France. Hereof by many prescriptions
was the Lady Elizabeth held accessory; which
the queen's Council would have examined and
chastised, but the king again protected her from
this danger. It was consulted that two Catholic
gentlemen should be sent to her to remain there
and observe what passed, and so were sent Sir
Thomas Pope and Mr. Robert Gage. But the
lady by her wary carriage, her courteous behaviour and cunning, and by her public profession
of Catholic religion with shew of zeal, did deceive
these gentlemen. Before the year was ended,
underhand she had intelligence with Mr. Thomas
Stafford, who then exiled in France suddenly
coming into England should title himself king,
(for that he was descended from the house of the
dukes of Buckingham) and should marry with
the Lady Elizabeth; they supposing themselves
strong enough against Queen Mary. It was
not long before Mr. Stafford put this in execution;
for coming out of France only with forty men on
24th April, 1557, and took Scarborough Castle, with
hope that either the Lady Elizabeth would send
her forces to fetch him, or with them to come to
him herself. But when by the diligence of the

Earl of Westmoreland he was intercepted, sent to London and beheaded, and some others of his faction hanged, the relics of this crime remained upon the Lady Elizabeth. It was her luck that at this time King Philip had returned from Flanders into England, by whose singular favour she again escaped this plunge.

Queen Mary in her last sickness sent Commissioners to examine her about religion, to whom she answered, "Is it not possible that the queen will be persuaded I am a Catholic, having so often protested it?" and thereupon did swear and vow that she was a Catholic. This is answerable to what Mr. Camden saith, and is likewise confirmed by the Duke of Feria's letter to the king, who in this sickness of the queen visited the Lady Elizabeth. He certified him that she did profess the Catholic religion and believed the Real Presence, and was not like to make any alteration for the principal points of religion.

Queen Mary's reign began 6th July, 1553. She returned all things that concerned the state of religion as her grandfather, King Henry VII., had left them, and as they had been continued by all Christian princes from the time when the

Christian religion entered into England. She abrogated all statutes of innovations and new devices during the time of her brother and father, reducing all to the humble obedience of the faith. She punished divers of the heads of those innovations that had been made; and above others, the chief author of all, Thomas Cranmer, who entering as a Catholic, as was supposed, into that dignity, was the first archbishop that ever failed in faith from the rest that were before him and from the obedience of the See Apostolic. This queen forgave the subsidies granted in the last year of her brother, gave great alms to the poor, remitted the debts of such officers of her house as she found burthened, restored more noble houses decayed than ever did prince in England, and brought with her peace and plenty. In a word, for magnaminity and virtue she was the worthiest princess that this kingdom ever had; and yet heresy had so enchanted the minds of divers of her subjects as in the five years of her reign she had more open and violent oppositions of her own subjects than Queen Elizabeth had in the forty-five years almost that she reigned.

Plain was the government of this queen, without tricks or new devices, severe to foul sinners against God and sharp to such as offended against the crown, to which she was more forced than by nature inclined. She was a great justicier, yet withal how merciful she was appeared manifestly by her gracious compassion to the Duchess of Somerset, to Sir John Cheke, Sir Edward Montague, Chief Justice, Sir John Cholmeley, the Marquis of Northampton, Sir Henry Dudley, Sir Francis Gates, the Lord Robert Dudley, and to the Duke of Suffolk;—all of them her professed enemies and most of them attainted, all adverse to her religion and no friends to her title; and yet she released them all out of the Tower, where they were prisoners.

Yet the Protestants were still busy against her and gave her no quietness. They libelled against the Government of Woman, published discourses and invectives against religion, and conspired her deprivation to advance her successor. All these sedicious actions had for their ground the religion then not fully six years old; a religion of mere liberty, most pleasing to gallants, void of all austerities. They cried her down because so many were burnt in her time; but she caused no new laws to be made against heretics but only recalled such as were used and of force in God's

Church since the Christian religion was established in England. And when in any did concur
the faults of heresy and treason, or felony, her
will was that the law should proceed, heresy
being directly offensive and immediately against
God.

Queen Mary having lived thirty-seven years a
maid, for the good of her country, to leave issue
married the noblest prince of Christendom, who
brought wealth, honour, and the best alliance in
Europe to the crown of England. Yet see what
treasons and conspiracies did follow. Sir Thomas
Wyat's rebellion in the east of England; Sir
Peter Carew, Sir Gawen Carew and Sir Thomas
Dennie in the west; Sir James Croftes and others
in Wales; the Duke of Suffolk (after he had
been pardoned) in Leicestershire. Then, after
that, the conspiracies of the Earl of Devonshire,
Sir Nicholas Throckmorton and others. And
William Thomas, who plotted to murder the
queen, being a secretary in King Edward's time;
who, when he was executed said he died for his
country. After this were Udall, Throckmorton
and others, with Thomas Stratford, of whom I
have touched before.

Queen Elizabeth succeeded in the kingdom on

17 November, 1558, king Philip being in France before Dourleus. She was persuaded by her new councillors to resume the spiritual power and jurisdiction. And it is probable that she was persuaded, seeing what she had vowed in the sickness of Queen Mary to the Commissioners that examined her, and what she told the Duke of Feria, and what she protested to ambassadors and divers others at several times often, as is noted by Catholic writers, who related divers particulars, as that she showed devotion to the Holy Cross, to our Blessed Lady and to the Saints. When she died she had next her body a crucifix of gold, hanging before her breast, so that Doctor Barlow said she died a Papist. Yet it seems that these men who would erect a new religion followed their own persuasions, and by little and little turned all upside down ; and by them she was drawn to make such grievous laws against Catholics as never prince before her did make against any malefactor whatsoever. And this is witnessed by the multiplicity of statutes yet extant, the death of so many priests and the affliction of innumerable subjects for that cause.

The queen before her Coronation put all bishops to silence and commanded they should not preach; and after the Parliament all that refused the oath were deprived of honours, livings and employments, either in Church or Commonwealth, and were committed to prison. There were in all of England fourteen bishops, most learned prelates, ten of Ireland, deposed; twelve deans, fifteen masters of colleges, six abbots, twelve archdeacons, one hundred and sixty priests, and Mr. Shellie, Prior of St. John's of Jerusalem.

The Communion Book, which was their new Church Service Book, was composed by Parker, Grindall, Horne, Whitehead, Bill, and Sir Thomas Smith. Was it ever known in a Christian kingdom that a course for religion was devised and framed without the consent and assistance of a bishop? But this was now done by these new upstarts and laymen, who afterwards made themselves bishops. In the disputations that followed the president appointed was Sir Nicholas Bacon, a mere layman, then made Lord Keeper. He being a great lawyer, but no divine, was one of the chiefest of them that persuaded the queen to take the course she did and to alter religion.

The end of the good bishops was this. Dr.

Scott, Bishop of Chester, died at Louvain in exile; Goldwell of St. Asaph at Rome; Pate of Worcester subscribed at the Council of Trent for the clergy of England, and never returned; Dr. Oglethorp of Carlisle, who consecrated the queen, died suddenly and shortly after his deprivation; learned and famous Tunstall died a prisoner at Lambeth; Bourne of Wells was prisoner to Carew, dean of the chapel; Thirlby of Ely was committed to the Tower and afterwards to Lambeth, where he died; Abbot Fecknam, Bishop Watson, Bishop White and Bishop Bonner died prisoners; and Prior Shelly in exile. This was the downfall of the Catholic clergy, a thing incredible to posterity.

The queen when she came to the crown was full twenty-five years of age, a gracious lady and gallant of aspect. Yet she would not be persuaded to marry, but would have it written on her tomb that she lived and died a virgin. King Henry the Fourth of France merrily said that the world would never believe this, nor would the many favourites she had, as Pickering, before she was queen, so as the world thought he should have married her. Nor would Leicester, nor Packington, nor Hatton, nor Rawley, nor Essex. To write all that might be said of her would fill many volumes. Mr. Camden in his Annals of her life has done it very partially, in many passages not telling all he ought to have done, and aggravating some passages, especially of Catholics. His conscience might tell him that all was not performed that he promised in his Epistle; and particularly in the relation of the proceedings, condemnation and death of the Queen of Scots, his majesty's mother, and the nearest kinswoman in blood the queen had, whose death was an eternal brand to our Queen Elizabeth. Yet her happiness is highly extolled by flattering heretics and such as know not, or will not know what passed before her reign, in her reign, and in her death. There was the ruin of many in her brother's and sister's time for her cause, the great distractions of her subjects' minds through the multitude of sects and differences in religion; the abundance of bloodshed of Catholic priests, honest men and of known integrity; the continual oppression of her subjects with subsidies and taxes; her assistance to other rebels against their natural princes, as the Hollanders and the Huguenots. There was that unjust law of the Supremacy to be

H

ministered to the people, the refusal of which by
them was treason, but not to be ministered to
the nobility.   Also her injuries done to the King
of Spain in taking his treasure, in permitting
some of her nobility to be commanders in matters
of piracy and robbery; permitting Drake and
others to rob his ships, spoil his towns, and
capture his people, she herself first giving cause
of hostility; thus much annoying him who was
three times the cause of saving her life and
redeeming her liberty.

But now to come to her death.   It grew of a
strange melancholy, very likely reflecting upon
the rehearsed particulars.   Now that she had
grown old her beauty was much decayed.   She
suspected that some of the greatest about her
looked towards Scotland.   These considerations
took from her all magnanimity.   Her negligence
in serving Almighty God suffered her to fall into
a distracted sadness and deep melancholy before
she died.   For before she fell very sick, being at
Whitehall her senses, appetite and rest decayed,
and she was troubled with fearful visions;
whereupon she removed to Richmond and fell
sick indeed.   She told a lady, one of the nearest
about her person, that she had seen a bright

flame about her, and asked her if she had not seen visions in the night. Growing more sick, she, all dressed, sat two days and three nights in her chair, and would be persuaded by none to go to her bed, or eat, or drink. Only the Lord Admiral persuaded her once to drink some broth, for to no other would she answer a word; but she said softly to him if he had known what she had seen in her bed he would not persuade her as he did. Commanding the rest of the lords to depart her chamber she willed the Lord Admiral to stay, to whom she shook her head and with a pitiful voice said to him "My Lord, I am tied with a chain of iron about my neck." He alleging her wonted courage she replied; "I am tied, and the case is altered with me."

There was discovered in the bottom of the queen's chair a card (the Queen of Hearts) with an iron nail knocked through the head of it, which the ladies durst not then pull out, thinking it to be some witchcraft. So the queen, growing past recovery, kept her bed some days. The Archbishop of Canterbury and some other prelates were sent to her, but she was much offended on seeing them; she cholericly rated them, and bid them be packing. Afterwards she exclaimed to

the Lord Admiral that she had the greatest
indignity offered to her by the archbishop that
a prince could have, to pronounce sentence of
death against her as if she had lived an atheist.
And some lords offering to send some other
prelates to her, she answered that she would
have none of those hedge-priests. So none came
to her until she was past sense and at the last
gasp, when they said some prayers not far from
her. Thus ended that great queen after forty-
four years, four months and a few days' reign in
great worldly glory and pleasure. It is not
known that in all this sickness she said "God
help me!" or any prayer or aspiration calling
on God or asking His mercy.

But now it is time, after this long digression,
to return to our lady duchess.

CHAPTER VII.

THE ARRIVAL IN ENGLAND OF THE DUKE OF FERIA. HIS HISTORY AND CHARACTER. HE MARRIES JANE DORMER.

WHEN King Philip, the Prince of Spain, came into England to marry the queen, many great personages and noble gentlemen did attend him, among whom was El Conde Don Gomez de Figueroa y Cordova, afterwards Duke of Feria, a great Lord and Grandee of Spain, much favoured by him and of his Council of State. This man began to look with particular affection upon the duchess, curious (as the Spaniard is) to know her birth, descent and quality. He finding both in antiquity and other titles of honour not to be inferior to his (although great men of Spain seldom marry out of their own rank and nation), intended to solicit a match, moved thereto by the favour she had with the queen, and the grace and beauty of her person. And this affection, as much grounded upon her virtuous parts as on the rareness of her beauty (the duke was then thirty-eight years of age), considering all the parts of this fair lady, esteemed him happy who should enjoy her. Which is an apparent argument of the worth, gentle and modest behaviour of the duchess, that not only the greatest of her own country, but of foreign nations did pretend her. And seeing it was the happiness of a stranger to obtain this pretence, he had the more obligation to esteem her, leaving country and friends and as good matches for his sake, which, as I noted before, the duke himself attested in his last will and testament. For which last will, having beseeched the king to be pleased that the duchess, the Lady Jane Dormer, his dear, most beloved and lawful wife, might choose two towns of his estate, with their jurisdictions, civil and criminal, and their whole rents and profits, wherewith she might entertain herself for the time that she should live. "And this, I am obliged " (saith he) "to ask of your majesty, because the duchess hath left the principal matches of her country and trusted in me a stranger, her servant and vassal." These are the words of the duke in his last testament. In this election of a husband, as in the course

and proceedings of her life, she imitated the virtue and prudence of the queen her mistress. For
when the queen, by the humble supplication of
the whole kingdom, and by the judgment and
advice of her wise and Catholic Council, intending to that which was most convenient for the
public good, determined to marry ; judging thereby, all matters as well for Religion as government might be better established by hopeful
succession. And albeit, divers were propounded
both within and without the kingdom, yet at last
the resolution was to have the marriage with
the Prince Philip of Spain, son to the Emperor
Charles V. as most honourable and beneficial to
the kingdom. So also the duchess preferred
before great lords at home, this noble stranger of
Spain, the duke of Feria. The king and queen
gave their willing consent for this marriage ; but
she would in no case have it solemnized until the
king's return from Flanders, whither the king
went about the wars which were made upon the
frontiers of France, and with him went the duke.

In the meantime the Queen fell sick, whereof
she died, to whom the king sent the duke to visit
her, but the king returned not. After the death
of the queen, and her funeral accomplished, the

duchess retired to her grandmother, who then lay at her house in the Savoy,[1] where the duke, prosecuting the desire of the marriage to be affected, it was solemnized in the church of the Savoy the 29th of December, being the feast of the renowned martyr St. Thomas of Canterbury. Although very unwilling, her uncles, the Earl of Sussex and Sir Henry Sidney, did agree to this marriage ; being distasteful to them to see such their niece of that esteem and regard to leave country, kin, and friends to go to live with a stranger in a country so far from them, and in a climate so different from theirs. But Almighty God had so ordained it, and the duke held it his happiness to be her husband, whom for her virtue and worth he prized, as he said, beyond all the states and professions of the world.

[1] The palace of the Savoy, the residence of the dukes of Lancaster, was wrecked by the mob in their hatred of John of Gaunt in 1381. It lay in ruins until Henry VII. by his last will gave it as an hospital for a master and four chaplains. Suppressed by Edward VI., it was revived by Queen Mary. Having a considerable portion of the building to spare, the Master seems to have been in the habit of letting it out as lodgings. The account of Dr. George Montague, in 1608, contains an entry which shews that Sir Robert Dormer then occupied the lodging formerly occupied by his grandmother. The early registers having been destroyed by a fire, no record of the marriage of the duke is to be found. See Newcourt, 1—696.

The duke was yet resident as ambassador and vicegerent of his king; and held his authority with great valour and wisdom ; and showed great zeal and devotion to Catholic Religion. For when the new queen began to alter and pervert the sacred office of the Church, to annihilate the ancient laws that touched Religion, which her deceased sister had renewed, the day that she should be crowned, the duke being earnestly requested from the queen and importuned by the Council to be present at her coronation (as he had been present when she rode through London and was installed queen,) he demanded, if in the coronation there would be performed all the usual ceremonies that were observed in the coronation of other Christian kings, according to the Catholic Church and ancient use of Catholic princes in this kingdom. And perceiving by their answer, there would be some alteration, he by no means would be entreated to assist there, neither publicly in the Church, nor in secret apart, or in a place that should be provided for him ; for that he would not authorize by his presence any act that gave not due observation to the honour and custom of the Catholic Church.

About that time came into England, for

Leger-Ambassador the Bishop of Aquila.[2] The
king, still remaining in Flanders, sent for the
Duke of Feria, who, before his departure out of
England, at the motion and instance of the
duchess his wife, by way of petition asked of the
queen to do him the favour to give him the
Religious, both men and women, of her kingdom
that would go with him; for that he would
procure to dispose them to such parts where they
might freely serve God and keep the rules of
their profession. He had before this tried all
possible ways to persuade the queen and her new
councillors not to change nor alter the Catholic
Religion which she found publicly professed
when she succeeded in the crown, but would
permit the laws established for it to stand in
force; promising by the power and assistance
of the king to clear all difficulties and resist all
oppositions. But all in vain, for what smooth
answers they gave they put in practice the
contrary. What he requested touching the
Religious to go out of England, he obtained,
although with grief and trouble of some of the

---

[2] Alvaro de Quadra, Bishop of Aquila, of whom many
notices occur in the Foreign Correspondence of the early years
of Queen Elizabeth.

principal councillors, who murmured and put in many stumbling-blocks to hinder it, alleging to the queen many inconveniences that might grow to herself and her proceedings by this permission. Notwithstanding the duke desisted not (such was his courage and zeal) pressing the queen with her word and promise, but got as many of them together as he could and would come to Durham house where he lodged, and there he sustained them until he procured their passage for Flanders. In which company were three convents; one of the Carthusian monks of Sheene,[8] who by the Providence of God remain yet an entire convent, at Mechlin in Brabant; another of nuns of the holy order of St. Bridget who were of Sion,[4] which monastery also yet remains whole, of many noble gentlewomen and blessed sisters at

[8] They had been reinstated in 1556. Twelve professed monks and three lay brothers, with their prior, Maurice Chauncey, left England and arrived in Flanders 1st July, 1559. They resided successively at Bruges, Louvain, Mechlin and Nieuport until their final dissolution by the Emperor Joseph II. in 1783.

[4] The MS. history of this convent, formerly belonging to the Earl of Shrewsbury states that "By means of the Duke of Feria the nuns obtained licence of the queen to depart in the first year of her reign, the said duke preparing a ship by order of King Philip for their secure passing the seas."

Lisbon in Portugal; a third was of St. Dominic's Order of the nuns of Dartford;[5] but being few, they were soon dispersed in monasteries of their own order. And when the duke went out of England, which was about the end of May, 1559, he had with him many priests, as afterwards in the train of the duchess followed many others. And being arrived where the king was he presented to his majesty their case, beseeching his favour and protection; which the king promised with great charity and piety, as became so great and Catholic a prince.

The duke left the duchess at his house in London, where she remained almost to the end of July; at which time Don Juan de Ayala,[6] sent by the king and duke for her, came to London. The duchess was presently to put herself in order for the voyage; and on the 24th of July she went to take the leave of Queen Elizabeth; and expecting in the presence-chamber, until the

---

[5] See on the history of this foundation Tanner's Not. Monast. p. 225.

[6] The credence given to John de Ayala on being sent to Queen Elizabeth in order to conduct the Countess of Feria into Flanders, is dated at Ghent, 9th July, 1559. See Calend. of Foreign Papers, No. 959. The queen's reply to Philip's letter is dated on the 25th of the same month. Id. No. 1060.

queen called for her, and staying long, the Spanish Ambassador began to be angry, desiring her either to sit down or to return, for she was now seven months gone with child. The bishop spake loud, seeing who she was and with child, that it was not fit she should stand there waiting, and would have pressed her to sit down in the chair of State. Which when the queen understood she presently came forth.[7] That compliment done, within two days following she took her journey towards Dover, where she was to be embarked. She went accompanied with a troop of noble gentlemen and ladies, her kin and friends, among whom was the Lord Bishop, Leger-Ambassador, who had special commandment from the king to have care of her. Also went with her the good lady, her dear and beloved grandmother, taking that opportunity to go where she might freely and securely serve God and

[7] A version of this story, intended for the guidance of Sir Thomas Challoner, the English ambassador at Madrid, was sent to him by Cecil in a letter dated 27th July. Of course it exonerates Elizabeth and places the conduct of the Bishop of Aquila in the most unfavourable light. Cecil speaks with respect of the Countess of Feria. See Foreign Papers of Elizabeth, 27th July, 1559, No. 1082. The farewell interview took place on the 23rd July.

enjoy the help and means for it. The duchess had attending on her six gentlewomen, the daughters of noble and principal gentlemen. One was sister to the Lord Harrington, her cousin-german; another sister to Sir Edward Stradling; another sister to Sir William Pickering, the queen's favourite; another was Mrs. Paston, who afterwards returning to England, was married to Sir Henry Newton of Gloucestershire, and became of the bed-chamber to Queen Elizabeth, and others; and with these Mrs. Clarentia, who from the childhood of Queen Mary had served her, and ever in principal place about her; a woman respected and beloved by the queen, who the rest of her life remained with the duchess. Besides the priests that were permitted to go over, divers gentlemen sheltered themselves under her protection, to go where they might according to their desire serve God.

Arrived at Dover, after taking leave of friends, where was the Earl of Sussex and Sir Henry Sidney, the next day after dinner she embarked for Calais, where within few hours she landed, received by Monsr. Gourden, governor of Calais, whither came also the governor of Boulogne to visit her. And after a day's rest and two nights,

having been very honourably entreated and
feasted by those governors in the town of Calais,
she took her journey for Graveling, thence for
Dunkirk, places subject to the King of Spain; in
both which she was received with extraordinary
great feasts and triumphs, discharging all the
artillery of the place. The governors meeting
her with their captains and soldiers marching in
military order, giving all signs of welcome entertainment, presenting her with gifts accustomed
in such places to noble personages.

From Dunkirk she passed Newport and came
to Bruges,[8] where she rested some days; whither
came the duke her husband to receive her and
Don Luys Mendes, sent by the king to visit her
and bid her welcome into those parts. Also
thither came Don Antonio de Toledo, brother to
the Duke of Alva, Commander of the Order of
St. John and Grand-Prior of Castille. In this
city (as in the rest), the magistrates and governors
of the places adjoining did her great honour by
their rich presents, and gave testimony of their

---

[8] Writing to Cecil on July 29th, Challoner reports that the
Countess of Feria had been princely met upon the way, and
would rest her in a Spaniard's house at Bruges. Foreign
Papers of Elizabeth, No. 1093.

respect to the duke and to her. The duke was to go to Flushing, whither he passed with haste to see the king embark himself for Spain.[9]

The duchess went from thence, her grandmother still with her, passing Ghent, where she was magnificently entertained, for Antwerp, where she was likewise received with great solemnity and honour; the whole city gathering to the gates and besetting the streets to behold her entrance, (which was princely) on horseback; and six maids of honour, also on horseback, attending her person. So guided through the principal streets, and lodged in the English house, where the English merchants had then their staple. From thence, she removed to Liége, for that the Duchess of Parma, the king's sister, then lady governess, lay at Mechlin, intending to stay there until she was delivered of child; but her highness the governess would in no manner permit it, but called her to Mechlin to have her by herself. So to give satisfaction she removed to Mechlin, where she was also received with extraordinary regard; the governess taking order that she should be lodged and every way accommodated, as it could not be more both

[9] See the Foreign Papers quoted above, No. 1174, 1175.

for her honour and content. Her lodging was in the Cardinal Granville's house, the Archbishop of Mechlin,[10] and being within the month of the time that she reckóned to be delivered of child; which happily was accomplished on the 28th of September, the vigil of St. Michael the Archangel and of all holy Angels, bringing him then into the world. He was called at his christening Lorenço, or Laurence, in Spanish Don Lorenzo de Figueroa y Cordova, Marquis of Villalva. In shew and resemblance he was an angelical child, who by his good natural disposition and more by the good education of his mother became so illustrious and memorable a prince in the world, whose worth and great parts are not only famous and renowned in Spain but in all Europe, thus giving notice to the world of his great wisdom, learning and valour.[11]

For the birth of this son, there were great feastings, masks, and jousts by the Spaniards and Italians; and after eight days the baptism was to be solemnized, at which the godfathers were

[10] Antoine Perrenot, Bishop of Arras, became Archbishop of Mechlin in 1561, and was created cardinal in the same year.

[11] On 29th September Challoner reported to Cecil the birth of the child. See Foreign Papers, No. 1393.

I

the Cardinal Granville and the Bishop of Tour-
nay; the godmothers were the Duchess of
Parma,[12] governess, and the Countess of Hoch-
straete,[13] (for the use then was there to have two
godfathers and two godmothers) which was performed in most honourable and princely manner.

When the child was borne to the church, first
were divers noble personages carrying such things
as are used in baptism, the candles, the basin
and ewer, the salt, the chrism, etc. Then
followed the eldest daughter of the countess-
godmother, who did bear the child, and the
younger daughter, both gorgeously apparalled,
who carried the train of the child's mantle.
Then next followed Madam Governess, and next
to her the other godmother, attended with all the
ladies and nobility of the Court. The child was
christened by the name of Laurence, the name
of his grandfather, Count of Feria and Marquis
of Pliego; it being the custom that the heirs of
this house retain, *alternis vicibus*, the names of
Gomez and Laurence for many ages.

[12] Margaret, wife of Alexander de Medicis, Duke of Florence,
and subsequently of Octavian Farnese, Duke of Parma.

[13] Apparently Anne de Rennenberg, wife of Philip de Lalaing,
who died 14th August, 1555. See Théatre Profane de Brabant,
11, 39.

CHAPTER VIII.

WHEN the solemnity of the christening was ended the duchess, for to recover strength, remained
at Mechlin to the beginning of March following.
Her grandmother then parted from her to settle
herself in Louvain, as hath been said. The duke
took of an Italian merchant in Antwerp fifty
thousand ducats, which he borrowed for the journey into Spain for himself, the duchess and the
child, then six months old. The duchess went
first to Brussels, where she was entertained with
extraordinary signs of congratulation, as in other
places where she entered. There she stayed until the first of April, A.D. 1560, on which day
(being the Monday before Palm Sunday) she, her
husband and the infant Marquis her son, began
their journey towards Spain, accompanied with
many noble gentlemen and their attendants,

among whom was Sir William Shelley, of the Order of St. John, Grand Prior of England. They had for their better commodity double provision; to wit, that the furniture which served this day was carried before to serve the second day following, so as their servants had all things beforehand, where they should lodge, in readiness.

When they came to the frontiers of France many noble personages came to receive them, and Mons. D'Oussons was sent by the king and queen to welcome them into the country and to conduct them to the court. And in every town where they lodged the keys were brought to the duke, to be master of them that night. Coming to St. Denis in the Holy Week they rested there until Easter Eve. That day, in the afternoon, they entered into Paris and were lodged in the Duke of Guise's house, who was the queen's uncle, where they remained the Easter holidays and were visited by many. After that they went on their journey towards Amboise, where the king and the queen regent and the queen's mother lay; the king then being Francis the Second, son of Henry the Second, and this queen was Queen Mary of Scotland, mother of King James, now king of Great Britain.

They being arrived at the court, the princes sent to welcome them, and the queen commanded to bring the duchess to her palace, having ordered to provide a lodging for her. No sooner was the duchess entered into the palace but the Queen Regent came presently to visit her, who beholding her beauty, the sweetness of her countenance and the good grace of her person—they are the queen's own words, which I have heard from her secretary and a gentlewoman, his sister, one of the two that were admitted to be present at her death, —who heard the queen divers times report it, was marvellously taken with her presence, and showed affection for her; as when wearing mourning for the death of the king, her father-in-law, she that day put it off, to honour the duchess, and clothed herself in white. She also entreated the duchess that she also would be apparelled after the French manner, which, to please the queen, she yielded to: and the queen would have her clothed in her presence, which her Majesty did put her hand to, taking in it very particular content, for she would mend what the women had done; and from that time the queen began to bear her so entire and intimate love as she continued to keep it to her death, with many remonstrances.

That day she was invited to eat at the queen's table, who commanded the guard of the Scots gentlemen to wait on her, and did her so many royal courtesies as she would have done to any strange princess that had been nearest of her blood. She brought her to the queen's mother, who very kindly treated her, and promised afterwards to visit her herself. At her departure she sent divers to accompany her to the borders of Spain, and required with great charge, as occasions fell out, that she might hear from her and she would not fail to answer her; yea, and to provoke her to write to her. This correspondence continued while they lived, the queen subsigning all her letters, " Your perfect friend, old acquaintance and dear cousin, Maria Regina." Divers of which letters I have seen, and have four or five of them by me, written all with the queen's own hand, very affectionate and respectful. This respect was evidently to be seen when the duke her husband died, the queen being then detained prisoner in England, in the year 1571. She desired that the duchess might come into Flanders; and wrote unto his Catholic Majesty beseeching him that it might be so with his license, for that the duchess living in Flanders would be much for the service of God's

Church and of her Majesty, and that she should
so enjoy better health, being a climate more
agreeable to her natural constitution than that
of Spain; and that the queen for her part
should receive great consolation to have her so
near herself, and in regard of her present afflictions she should reap thereby both comfort and
benefit. And to this end did her Majesty also
write to his Holiness, commanding his ambassador
to solicit it very seriously as a matter very convenient to his service and her solace; and likewise to deal with the Ministers of his Catholic
Majesty, that the journey of the duchess to
Flanders might take effect. This the Queen of
Scotland desired exceedingly to accomplish, as
her secretary,[1] who wrote these letters, hath related
to me, a man very prudent and Christian, who
lived and died a very virtuous and pious Catholic;
for I am witness to both, having familiarly been
acquainted with him for almost six years, and by
him daily in his last sickness and present at his
death; a little before which, calling Father Creswell and the gentlemen and men of any fashion,

---

[1] A marginal note in the MS. tells us that this was " Monsr.
Gilbert Curle, secretary more than twenty years to the Queen
of Scots."

both English and Scots, he there protested upon
hope of his salvation, of his fidelity and true loyal-
ty ever to the queen, his mistress, both living
and dead, against the calumnies and imputations
put in print, the authors being too lightly credulous.
And this he spake (myself being a witness) with
great asservation, protesting his innocence ever
at the last gasp as he should answer it before the
tribunal of the Eternal Judge.   This I hold myself bound in conscience to write ; for that he desired all the assistants to witness what he affirmed
upon his death-bed.   The queen spake often of
the duchess, uttering words of great affection, much
commending her virtue and worth.   But this
desired journey could not take effect by reason of
the minority of her son.

But to proceed with the duchess' journey.
They arrived in Spain with good health, and
about the end of June came to Segovia, the king
and queen being then at a house of recreation in
the woods adjoining ; but the court then resided
in Toledo, to which place was referred the
journey of the duchess for their majesties.   Into
which city she entered the 9th of August, the
vigil of St. Laurence, 1560, with that honourable
lustre and unusual greatness that the houses of

the whole city were dispeopled to behold her
entrance. The king and the duke her husband
stood together in a window to see her pass, she
riding on horseback; the furniture of her horse
being of crimson velvet garnished with studs and
fringe of gold, and another horse led by, very
richly appointed. Her six dames likewise were
all alone on horseback, with velvet furniture,
suitable alike. The duchess had attending on
her twenty pages, all in costly liveries, and was
accompanied with most of the gallantry of the
court. But her own person graced all. The
king, before she visited the queen, came himself
to see her, to bid her welcome to the court of Spain.

The next day she went to kiss the queen's
hands, who was the eldest daughter of France;[2]
and so could give her account of the queen her
mother, the king her brother, his queen and the
other princes, her brothers and sisters; in whose
court she had been so honourably entertained.
The queen received her with much shew of kindness and favour, as much admiring her beauty as
envying her nation; and she gave her a jewel for
her welcome. The king of Portugal[3] sent of

---

[2] Isabella, daughter of Henry II., King of France.
[3] Sebastian, King of Portugal, from 1557 to 1578.

purpose to visit her, and to give her the Bien-
venida into those countries, and withal a fair
jewel for a present, which I have seen; and it
was valued by the jeweller at 8,000 ducats. For
some days these visits of welcome continued.
The respect of the duke her husband, the ·report
of her virtue and the comeliness of her presence
drew a regard and honour to her of the whole
court, by all performances, in such noble and
extraordinary manner as the memory thereof remains much extolled, especially among the kindred, allies and vassals of that house of Feria and
Cordova.

After that the duchess had rested in the Court
she repaired to *Zafra,* the duke's house on his
own estate in Estramadura, where she was received by the neighbouring gentlemen and tenants with such tokens of honour as could not
be greater nor more costly. Here now she begins
to put in practice the state of a married wife.
And although by the means of heats of that
country, so different from this where she was
born and brought up, she had so little health as
she was in a sort unfit to intend to anything besides
her prayers and her health; yet now being in her
own house she resembles her grandmother, of

whom she would be a perfect follower, seeking to treasure up in herself the degrees and excellencies of a good and perfect wife; so that her husband found in her a general treasure for all cares and chances. In all times and all occasions she sought to please him and increase his content-ment. For in mirth, the duchess was to him sweet and pleasing company; in matters of discontentment he found in her a lively comfort; in doubts a faithful and able counsellor; in adverse accidents a solace. All that knew them, knew how much the duke esteemed her, how dearly he loved her; for all those qualities he acknowledged to be in the duchess, as such as served them (and not in mean place) have attested to me with particular relation.

But for more complete testimony hereof is his last will and testament, wherein he distinctly remembereth those great parts in her, leaving her the only tutoress of their son and the gover-ness of his estate, until the time by the law made he was capable thereof, which is at twenty-five years of age; he being not full twelve years when his father died. For among other words in his testament of her praise, he hath these; " I be-seech of the duchess no particulars,—for that I

know what belongeth to the bringing up of her
son and the government of his lands, goods and
house, she will do much better than I do know to
ask it, etc." Withal charging his son, upon his
blessing and under pain of his curse, to love and
obey her; and telling him the great obligation she
had to her more than to a mother. As she was
to her husband, a respecting, loving and provident wife; so to her son she was a careful
mother, notable instructor, and a most prudent
tutoress. Her care gave him those principles
and foundations of wisdom, virtue and excellence,
wherewith he so shined and flourished in the
world as is singularly expressed in the funeral
oration at the solemnity of his funeral at *Zafra*.
Her prudent education instilled in him the
beginning and entrance to know how to govern
himself and others; for when upon the death of
his father, the king gave him the Encomienda [4]
of Segura de la Sierra, one of the richest in
Spain, which his father had before him, when he
had taken the habit of Santiago, she caused him
to go to the monastery of Santiago at Urles,
according to the custom of the Order, and would
not take dispensation for him, as others of his

[4] A grant or benefice attached to a military order.

quality do, but that he being young should perform his noviceship; which he did some months in serving Mass and performing other duties that he might the better know his obligations to God's service; at times, taking the recreations of so great a person. This education brought him to the fame and deserved renown he had in the world.

She was in her family a lady that gave remedy to their wants; cause of exercise and employment both to menservants and women according to their quality, detesting idleness, being herself a rare example of industry, piety, and imitable government.

About five years after her marriage she had another son, whom in baptism they called Don Pedro, after his great-grandfather by the grandmother's side. But this child had not accomplished three months when it pleased God to take him again.

It would ask a large discourse to relate the many memorable acts of the Christian zeal of this duchess while she was a married wife; but I will content myself in proof and testimony hereof to repeat what a great author doth affirm and hath published in print.

Fra Juan Baptista Moles, a Recollect Des-
calced of the Order of St. Francis, in his
Memorial that he wrote of the same province,
observes as followeth:[5] "The said Dukes of
Feria are, and have always been, patrons of this
house, who ordinarily repair hither and supply
with liberal hand the necessary occasions of the
same, accounting this house for their particular
recreation, in which they have a lodging (which
I have seen) where commonly, when they reside
in *Zafra*, they retire themselves in Lent, and for
the Holy Week, and other principal feasts of the
year. With the most singular devotion this did
the great duke, Don Gomez, first Duke of Feria,
and the most Christian duchess his wife, the
Lady Jane Dormer, a marvellous devotee of our
habit and religion. They, recollecting themselves
in this house, did not only give to the religious
to eat; but on Holy Thursday and other special
days, they with their own hands did serve; giving
them their meat in the refectory, and imparting it
to them with so great humility and affection as if
they had done it to the Apostles of Jesus Christ.
Afterwards they themselves, eating with the
lay friars and treating them with great devotion

[5] Memorial de San Gabriel, cap. xlii. Marg. Note in MS.

and plainness, left herein great edification to the
religious, and a marvellous example for such like
honourable persons. And so to this day liveth,
and shall live for ever, the memory of this so
pious and devout a lord among the religious, to
commend his soul to God and to pray for the life
of the duchess his wife, now a widow, who with
great example and praise of her holy behaviour,
continueth in the recollection of a very holy life;
who having been visited by God with the loss of
so worthy a husband, aparted from her country
and nation; yet remaineth in solitariness, as she
that is descended of noble and honourable blood
in the kingdom of England; still having in
remembrance this religious house de la Lapa;
and providing for it and for the rest that are in
her son's estate with such relief, alms and works
of charity, as one very intimately devoted to this
holy province and to the religious of the same."
This the said author, Fra Juan Baptista Moles,
writeth in his said Memorial; and in another
chapter following he saith further that the duke
and duchess did found and build the monastery
of our Lady de Monte-Virgine, situated half a
league from the town of Villalva. And that
after the duke's death his duchess, the Lady

Jane Dormer, builded the church in a very seemly and sumptuous fashion, for the great devotion that this princess had to this house.

In these and such like works of charity and sanctity did the duchess pass her married life, renowned as well for her wisdom, prudence and generous carriage in all accidents as in her devotion and zeal to religion, constant in good purposes, not dismayed with troubles, valorous in adverse chances and discreet in all excesses; shewing herself in all the worthy daughter of her parents and the wife of such a husband.

CHAPTER IX.

OF THE SICKNESS AND DEATH OF THE DUKE OF FERIA, HER HUSBAND.

To make yet further proof of the virtues of the duchess and to try her constancy and patience, it pleased Almighty God to allay and utterly dissolve the content of her married life, depriving her of that she best loved under heaven, giving the duke a fever so ardent and violent, as within twenty days he departed this life, it being the feast of the Nativity of our Blessed Lady early in the morning at the Escurial, when the king was there building his admirable, sumptuous, and royal house of St. Laurence, the 8th of September, 1571, having been married twelve years, eight months, and ten days.

This infirmity, what sensible grief and heaviness it impressed in the duchess, who so much honoured and so dearly loved him, may well be gathered by what he was and what she was; she

J

being a stranger, young, out of her country, far from her friends, left in a manner wholly solitary, with the care and charge of the estate of the duchy in her only son, not yet twelve years of age.

Here might be amplified her attendance and diligence towards the duke in this sickness, the entire love and affection wherewith she served him, her great solicitude to regale him, to help him, to inquire after expert physicians and seek for remedies that might procure health; the continual labour she passed night and day, present at all hours to assist in what was needful, and to give contentment in all occasions. But human pains or diligence availed little either of wife or king (who sent of purpose to Guadaloupe for a physician) nor of kin nor of friends, nor of servants; for, all seeing and feeling their loss failed not to procure and do what they could for his health and recovery. The time was come that it pleased God that this good duke should leave this vale of misery, to live with the blessed Saints, there to receive the eternal reward of his merits, whereof living and dying he gave hopeful assurance by many evident and most Christian effects.

I might here declare the valour, wisdom and understanding and other excellent parts of this great duke, which were so notoriously apparent to the world where he lived; but I rather desire to pass them with silence, than by my inability not to give them their deserved right and honour; for with his death failed one of the noblest and best gentlemen that the kingdom of Spain had or knew in his time, or since then to this day, which is manifest by the many great and important affairs wherein from his youth he was employed both in peace and war. The regard that the Emperor Charles the Fifth had of him, commending him as a notable and able assistant to Philip his son, and the esteem and favour that he held with this king to his death, being of his Council of State, Captain of his Spanish Guard; called always by his majesty to his private consults and intimate conferences, which as a most noble true gentleman and worthy counsellor he applied not to his own interest, little respecting increase of his own lands and wealth, but the honour of his king, the service of his country, the benefit of the common-weal and the advancement of such as merited. Noble personages and honourable widows who were fallen into wants,

made suit to this good duke as their patron and
best advocate, and found help for their necessities. Yea, it was very ordinary with him,
when strangers, were they English, Flemings,
or Italians, (especially if they were of quality,)
having suits and pretentions in the court, their
business requiring some time for examination,
(who often had much delay before they could be
despatched); this duke in the meantime gave
them allowance to sustain them; in so much
as when his steward made complaint that money
came not in to supply so much, and that he
wanted to provide what was necessary for his
own house; the duke would answer: "I have
plate, pawn it; and let not these men lack;"
compassionating their cases when their des-
patches were delayed. He preferred the affairs
of the public weal before his own, were they
never so important.

The duchess herself told me, that the duke
and she talking in private and discoursing of the
sudden rising and great wealth of some that had
the king's ear and were in his favour; she object-
ing the little increase that the duke had made,
yet no man more in favour, no man more
constant, no man more intimate with the king

than he, seeing most businesses of estate were passed and despatched by his means ; — he answered : " Would you that I take gifts and bribes, or that my honour remain in the point it doth, and should ? For if I would accept presents and gifts, you must cause the back door to be opened to pass them out ; for your house would quickly be so full as it would not contain them. But to this day my honour hath not been touched with bribes, and shall I now begin ? " She replied : " If it concern your honour, in God's name let it be ; for to uphold your honour, I had rather be poor than give way to the least decay thereof."

He was affable and sweet in condition, not haughty, no despiser, not proud, used all with marvellous courtesy and a continuing liberality where there was need. The respect he had to ecclesiastical and religious persons was notable ; his zeal and fervour in observance of the Catholic Religion were admirable. He rather suffered the displeasure of his mother, whom he ever observed with all duty and obedient respect, and the hazard to lose that great estate of the marquis-ship of Pliego, whereof his mother was heir, than he would consent to marry the only daughter of his elder brother Don Pedro, who died young, leaving no other issue, being so near of his blood; whom his mother (otherwise a most virtuous lady) in revenge married to his younger brother and put the estate in process between the two brothers.

While his sickness lasted, which daily grew more dangerous by the violence of the fever, he disposed all matters as a Christian should do, confessed, received the Sacraments of the Holy Eucharist and Extreme Unction; had always about him religious men, spent the time as his sickness might permit, in spiritual discourses; comforting the duchess, setting before her eyes the will of Almighty God that all must obey; her own Christianity and discretion, and so to suffer with patience his departure, leaving as a pledge their son who should supply his place. And then he called his son and gave him his blessing; he charged him to serve God, to live virtuously, to honour and obey his mother, repeating to him the great duty he did owe her. He was very devout to our Blessed Lady; and so on the day of her birth, he was born to God.[1]

[1] Namely, on the festival of the Nativity of our Blessed Lady, 8th September, 1571.

The king felt his death so heavily as he shed
tears; which is said he was never seen to do for
any but for his son Don Carlos. But this heavy
loss most touched the duchess in her particular,
although it was general, both for the king's
services, the benefit of his country, and for the
causes and pretensions of the good and well-
deserving, both subjects and strangers, religious
and secular.

He was a great furtherer and advancer of the
Fathers of the Society of Jesus (a Religion that
hath merited so well by their great labours,
learning, and good example, in the Church of
God) as Father Ribadeneira in his Epistle
(dedicated to the duchess) of his book *De los
Santos Extravagantes*,[2] confesseth in these words:
"It is long since that I have desired some good
occasion to declare unto the world the obligations
that all this little Society of Jesus hath to serve
your excellency and your most honourable house;
and I more than any, in regard I am so ancient
a witness of the many and singular favours we
have received from the hands of the most

---

[2] P. Ribadeneyra Epist. a Dona Juana Dormer, Duquesa de
Feria, 15 de Julio 1608. See De Backer, Bibl. des ecrivains de
la Compagnie de Jesus, iii. 154, ed. 1876.

excellent Lord Don Gomez de Figueroa y
Cordova, Duke of Feria,[8] your husband, and
which your excellency and the Duke Don
Lorenzo your son have always continued as true
lords, patrons, and defenders of our Society.
And for to say something of much that may be
said, in the year 1555 I went to Rome from
Flanders, sent by the blessed Father Ignatius,
our Father and Founder, for to be a suitor to his
Catholic Majesty to give us license to erect
colleges of the Society in those states, and there-
with to serve our Lord with our poor labours ; as
by His grace, the Society doth in so many other
parts of the world. Which petition, although it
were very just, yet it had many and most sore
difficulties and contradictions of such persons
as had more obligation to favour and assist so
holy a work (as it falls out in the like for God's
service) which the Duke Don Gomez, by his
authority, valour, and wisdom, made plain and
obtained of the king all that I pretended. For,
as he was so great a lord, and so great a favourite
of his majesty, and brother to Father Antonio
de Cordova, who was of our Society, and son of
the most worthy Lady Donna Catalina Fer-

---

[8] See Hist. Societ. Jesu, by Orlandini, p. 402, ed. 1620.

nandez de Cordova, Marquesa de Pliego, and brother of the Lady Donna Maria de Toledo, Duchess of Arcos, who were notable protectors of our Society and founders of the colleges of Montilla and Marchena, his Excellency undertook my protection ; and for the time that I remained in that court he was my defence, advocate, solicitor, powerful lord and loving father. He effected that which seemed impossible, and opened the door that stood so locked, that the Society might have houses and colleges in all those states. And by virtue of that license and privilege, it hath at this day more than twenty, and in them more than seven hundred persons in the most principal cities and towns of the Low Countries ; which much serve our Lord, illuminating and repressing heretics, animating Catholics, and instructing them to live Christianly, to obey God and their princes. And all this fruit, after our Lord, Who would be served with it, the Society oweth to the duke, as to the root from whence it sprung."

And afterwards in the same Epistle he addeth further, that in the year 1557 returning another time from Rome to Flanders, " I received," saith he, " many benefits and the whole Society in my

person. And I went with his Excellency into
England in the year 1558, sent by the king to
assist in the infirmity of our lady and queen,
Queen Mary, etc."

Moreover, in the death of this duke, our country
and Catholics lost a main and evident hope of
their desire for the restitution of the Catholic
religion, knowing his zeal to further all means
and helps that might effect this restitution by
that which appeared he did in the beginning of
the change at his coming out of England; and
partly by undertaking the government of the
Low Countries, which was appointed to him in
the year 1571. He provided for the journey;
but then his mortal sickness seizing upon him, it
pleased God to alter this expected happiness. I
have been credibly informed that more than once
he hath with hearty instance insinuated to the
king that the relief of our country imported
much the reputation of his majesty; and that
before God and man he was bound in honour to
give remedy, seeing the ruin thereof came upon
his relinquishing it, his good queen and wife
having settled it in so good estate. And that
his majesty could not forget what passed, he
being employed by him as his counsellor and

servant to preserve her that then stood and ruled; and contrary to hope and promise had confounded all. And that the duke had this zeal to our country appeareth by sundry letters written after his death in the Latin tongue to his majesty and to the duke, his son, wherein also appeareth the respect and esteem that the English Catholics had to the lady duchess, desiring that she might come into the Low Countries. This letter I found written with a most fair and legible hand, and subscribed with these names; namely, Doctors William Allen, Owen Lewis, Thomas Stapleton, Richard Hall, Richard White, William Carter, William Smith, William Knott, John Dauley, Licenciates, or Bachelors of Divinity; Henry Joliff, William Taylour, Thomas Wilson, Thomas Bailie, Laurence Webbe, Peter Foster, Cuthbert Vaux, Thomas Metham, Thomas Parker, Thomas Dorman, Giles Capell, Gregory Bell, Gilbert Branford, Edmund Hargatt, Thomas Hide, John Marshall, John Fenne, Thomas Freeman, Maurice Chancy, prior of the Carthusians, for him and his convent. This letter to his Catholic majesty was dated at Antwerp on 6th October, 1571.

A letter from the same writers to the Duke of

Feria on the death of his father was written on
the same day.

Another from the same to the Cardinal Protector was carried by Dr. Nicolas Sanders.

His Holiness Pope Pius Quintus did write
unto the duchess upon the news of the death of
the duke, which brief is dated at St. Peter's,
28th November, 1571, and subsigned, Ant.
Buccapedalius.

CHAPTER X.

OF THE WIDOWHOOD OF THE DUCHESS AND HER VIRTUOUS EXERCISES IN THAT ESTATE.

THE duchess now in the eighteenth[1] year of her
marriage and thirty-fourth of her age, beset on
every side with the divers and heavy thoughts of
her widowhood, the present solitariness and the
heavy memory of her past contentment, yet so
moderated her passions (which commonly in
such accidents, even in the wisest, grow to

[1] Read, "the thirteenth." In the margin of the original
occurs this note,

"For the virtues of a widow read the fortieth chapter of
Francis of Sales, Bishop of Geneva, his *Introduction to a Devout
Life,* which our duchess practised before he wrote it."

extremes, affection over-ruling discretion, such is the force of these passions beyond reason) as considering all circumstances which I must repeat, yet so young, a stranger, so far from country and friends, her loss so important, must needs augment grief; and the more for that there was no remedy, for recovery; nevertheless, necessity did not persuade so much a moderation as religion directed to look upon her husband rather absent than dead; whereupon she resolveth a constant purpose to hold true fidelity to him and together to conform herself to the will and ordinance of God Almighty.

The duke in his death-bed recommended to this lady especially three things—his soul, his son, and his honour. His soul to be prayed for and assisted with the holy Sacrifice of the Church, alms-deeds and other good works of charity; his son to be brought up christianly, in the fear of God, learning and qualities answerable to his rank and condition; his honour to be taken care of, to pay his debts, and make satisfaction where it was due. Of all which she had so particular care as she neither slacked time, nor omitted opportunity with all speedy accomplishment to pay this performance as was requisite.

As concerning the first; presently upon his
death, in all the monasteries and parishes about
the Escurial and in Madrid, large alms was given
to pray for his soul. And in the duke's estate,
in many Religious houses, perpetual memories
were founded to this end. And the duchess to
her death did always continue the remembrance
of this charge where she lived ; and in her will,
left particular charge, to the duke her grandson
always to accomplish the aidful memory of his
grandfather, father, and hers ; observing with
special solemnity his anniversary rites; which
charge she commended to myself for divers years,
to be done in most of the monasteries of Madrid
with good alms.

For the second, which was the education of her
son, is showed before in the description of his
life and worthy parts.

And the third to uphold his honour in paying
his debts and in giving satisfaction where aught
might be with conscience required, and in main-
taining the honourable estate of his house, she
notably showed the effects of a loving wife and
the affectionate memory of a most christian, in-
dustrious and provident lady. For at the death
of the duke, his estate (for his own debts and the

debts of the Count Don Pedro his elder brother,
contracted for the service of their princes), stood
engaged to the value of 300,000 ducats, which
this good lady by her provident government in
her time cleared.   For when the duke her grandson entered into it, he found it free and discharged.   He being employed to do the obedience to
Pope Paul the Fifth, being the first employment
and he young, would perform it with extraordinary
greatness, and so put himself into a new engage-
ment for that embassage, which was very little,
considering how his grandmother found it when
his grandfather died.   This her government was
not by withdrawing any allowance that touched
the maintenance of her house or honour of her
son ; or by new inventions or tricks to oppress her
vassals or tenants, whom always she entreated
with such sweetness and plausible proceedings as
they extraordinarily respected, reverenced and
affected her.   Which to demonstrate, one example among many may make plain.

It happened in the year 1603 that the king
made offer to farm out the tollage that was by
Badajoz, upon the confines of Portugal.   The
duke, her son, was the viceroy of Sicily ; who,
advertised of this farming, wrote presently to his

mother to take it for him, whatsoever it cost, because joining to his estate, it lay convenient for
him and more for him than any, and very prejudici-
ally and hurtful if any other should rent it. Which
the duchess receiving, presently sent to the king's
office accepting the farm, desiring to know the
price. It was replied forty thousand ducats; and
this same to be paid in few days all in ready
money; and to be paid as the order was before the
estate could be passed. The duchess put to this
exigence presently to provide so much money, living in Madrid, the Court being then at Valladolid
(almost one hundred miles off) where the money
was to be paid, by the assistance of a friend, she
presently had lent her fourteen thousand ducats.
For the rest, which was twenty-six thousand
ducats, she presently despatched a messenger,
writing to Zafra to the governor of the duke's
estate to call the tenants and solicit them for
this sum, showing the necessity of present payment, and promising by her letter repayment
within four months. The messenger came to Zafra
about eleven o'clock before noon. The governor having read the duchess her letter, sent his
man presently to most of the principal of the town
to meet him at the town-house at two o'clock;

in which place they assemble at the same hour.
The governor read to them the duchess's letter,
and so requested their answer. And this followed:
that by seven o'clock the same evening the whole
twenty-six thousand ducats were brought to the
governor's house without any further reply, or request of more security of bills or bands than the
promise of the bare letter that she wrote. This
the governor himself reported to me, admiring it
when we were at the solemnity of her funeral.
Such was the love and respect the tenants had
always to her, albeit a stranger; having merited
it by her affable and excellent government.

CHAPTER XI.

THE MODE OF LIFE OF THE DUCHESS DURING
HER WIDOWHOOD.

THE duchess for her own private entertainment
gave herself wholly from the death of her husband
to a recollected kind of life, putting from her all
ostentation of greatness, both in attendance,
apparel, and house-furniture, as usually all
widows of respect do in Spain. She, always
upholding what was necessary for the service of
her son and the managing of his estate, wholly
employed her time in virtuous exercises, serving
Almighty God in works of piety; wherein to her
death she so exemplarly continued as that all
sorts, both religious and secular, the greatest
and the meanest, had her in respect and
reverence.

So likewise was her house governed. Holiness
at home; courage abroad; prudence everywhere.
Her servants were provided of all things neces-

sary according to their place, office, and merit;
their rations and wages always paid most
punctually. In sickness or other infirmities, her
regard and severe commandment to have the
physician called, were the sick man the meanest
in her service; and orderly to be provided and
given whatsoever the physician appointed. She
gave leave and special charge to all her servants
daily to hear Mass; and when Mass was read
every day in her own oratory her care was that
all her women servants should be present at the
beginning; for the men-servants might go abroad
to church. Very exact was her order that all
her family should go to confession on all the
solemn feasts of the year, and likewise the feasts
of our Blessed Lady. That they should be
advised to keep the Commandments of God and
of His holy Church; should be friends of truth,
extremely abhorring the contrary; should live in
peace; be chaste and honest in their comportment; for the shew of the contrary in any
gesture or condition did much offend her. Yea,
she did so govern her house and family as she
may be a notable example for others to follow.
By her careful providence, disengaging her house,
as hath been said, of such great debts as lay

upon it; and breeding up her son with that noble
and virtuous education, as hath been also declared.   Her service was a school and pious
nursery of virtue and an exemplar to all that had
the happiness to serve her; for divers of them
left the world and became religious.   I think
that during the forty years she lived a widow,
few passed that some or other went not out of
her house into religion, as I knew divers that
had been her servants of the Order of St. Francis,
both Descalços and others; some of St. Dominic's
Order, some Augustines, Benedictines, Jesuits, and
others.   Thus was her house and family governed.

The second virtue of St. Paul's widow is, to
honour and have great respect to parents.   According to the next and strict literal sense the
duchess had no matter to perform this counsel;
for that before she was a widow, her grandfather,
grandmother and mother died, and her father
soon after, who was in England married to
another wife and had divers children, and she in
Spain.   But while he lived she was not unmindful
to offer and present the respect that did become
her; and for the deceased, her prayers and the
Sacrifice of the Church, which she had care
should be offered for their souls, were testimony

of her love and honour to them; giving large alms to particular monasteries only for this office. And the former course of her life (namely to her grandmother who brought her up,) is a plain evidence how mindful she was of this duty; over whose body (which lieth in the choir before the high altar in the Charterhouse of Louvain) together with her sister, the Lady Hungerford, she caused a fair tomb to be erected; and gave to the monastery a hundred florins of rent for ever. But if the parents live not (whom she may corporally serve, assist, and cherish), this counsel may fitly be applied to their souls; for widows rarely see their parents live, being for the most part parents themselves.

In her love and regard to the duke her son, and likewise to his son, her grandchild, when he was young and capable of instruction, her care and vigilance were more than ordinary or natural; for no occasion might make her omit her virtuous advices and admonitions (yea, even when they were men and married) to serve God and live virtuously. And for example among many, this passed in mine own hearing. When the duke that now is, her grandson, was honoured with the knighthood and habit of St. James, and

solemnly invested in the church of St. Dominic
in Madrid; the solemnity being done, he coming
to his grandmother the duchess (for her house
was near to it) with his red cross on his breast,
she congratulating his new honour spoke to him
in effect these words : " Son, you are now a new
man ; for in taking this habit, you are entered
into many new obligations ; and all are to bind
you to be a faithful and valorous knight in the
service of Almighty God and His Church.   This
cross upon your breast is to put you in remembrance under Whose banner you serve, and
Whose soldier you are ; and so a motive to have
Him always before your eyes Who by His death
made the Cross honourable, as you have it for an
honour to wear it where you do.   And since that
His greatest enemy is sin, it is your part to fight
and war always against sin ; for otherwise it will
be but false dealing to bear His colours and yield
to His enemy.   Good son, reflect upon this, and
do your best to put it in practice, and you will be
honoured both of God and men.   And so God
Almighty give you the joy I wish you with it."
And then she kissed his cheek.   And so with
tenderness on both sides she gave and he took
her blessing upon his knee.

The Lady Hungerford, as hath been said, was her only sister by father and mother, who married with an unkind husband. She being oppressed by him for her conscience, with his permission, in 1571, came over into Flanders ; where being ill-paid (or not at all paid,) that which was promised and was due to her from her husband, and too much neglected by her friends in England, found to her death the cherishing love of her sister the duchess in so favourable and continuing bounty with great affection, as she deducted from her own maintenance to assist her, as I know and have seen by many specialties performed to her, both in life and death.

Among others that attended the duchess out of England was Mrs. Margaret Harrington, sister to the Lord Harrington, her cousin german. She married her to a noble gentleman of worth, Don Benito Cisneros, and gave her in dowry twenty thousand ducats. She at her death, acknowledging the great favours and bounty she had received from the duchess, (having before buried her husband and two children she had by him,) for gratitude, with her means remaining, founded in Zafra the greatest part of a monastery of religious women of the holy Order of St. Francis, where her body lies buried. The duchess being in the estate of widowhood for so many years and in the many troubles that happened, such as sickness and other temporal crosses, to such as were dearest unto her; in all, ever shewed great example of Christian patience and confidence in Almighty God; and particularly in the death of the duke, her only son. Hereof I was an eye-witness. By his death she was not only left without a son, but without any living or estate in the world to maintain her. For her allowance, by her own request and assignment, was allotted her out of the Encomienda[1] of Segura, which, the duke dying, fell into the king's hands, wholly to be disposed where the king pleased. And with the heavy news of the duke's death, she not knowing his testament, nor what he might appoint for her, now seventy years of age, in a strange country, deprived of her son, wholly destitute of living, and without notice of any certain means for the sustenance of her and her family, yet fainted not in the trust of her certain Refuge, commending all to His Divine Providence, saying confidently: "Lord, Thy holy Will be done." But the duke had ordained and com-

---

[1] Already explained, see p. 124.

manded that she should be supplied and provided for to content, charging his son to fulfil it.

The persecution of Catholics in her country was a great affliction to her; that many times with tears and hearty compassion did she hear and report their troubles; yet her resolution was ever, saying, "Let us hope and trust in God; He will deliver us. The conversion of our country will be God Almighty's own work; therefore whosoever goes about upon their own valour, learning, devices, inventions, or any practice whatsoever to reduce it, as stealing the honour from God to this their drift and invention, it will not succeed. Our sins made the ruin, but God must and will restore the building. In the meanwhile let us hope and trust in His Divine mercy, expecting His heavenly pleasure, not omitting to pray daily and implore His goodness, and other good men to use their labours and learning to win souls, as out of foreign seminaries they have happily begun." A worthy speech and resolution in the trust of Almighty God.

CHAPTER XII.

THE ARM OF THE DUCHESS IS BROKEN. HER
SUBSEQUENT ILLNESS. HER ORDINARY MODE
OF LIFE DURING HER WIDOWHOOD.

UPON St. Bernard's day, the 20th of August,
1609, the Duchess of Infantadzo, coming to visit
her, the Duchess of Feria received her in the
hall, they both contending to give in courtesy
each other the precedence, our duchess carrying
her left arm in a scarf by reason of a pain she
had in her breast on that side, (for that the
stirring of her arm might not offend her breast,
which also was much weakened, the pain of the
breast decaying the strength of it,) the Duchess
of Infantadzo taking her by that hand would put
her before her; which doing with some force, the
other pulling her arm back, so wrested between
both, broke the bone a little above the elbow; at
which suddenly our duchess gave a sighing groan,
saying " *Mi braço està quebrado*" (My arm is

broken). I, being the next before the duchess, astonished at the sudden cry and complaint, not imagining it could be broken with so small a violence, rather thinking it might be put out of joint, called her women, who came to her, and taking her arm affirmed the same. The pain being extreme, servants were sent with all speed to find a bone-setter, and advised to a lame one who was said to be skilful. The first found came to her, took her in hand, and said it was broken; but the unskilful fellow, lame of both his legs, handled her very roughly. She was forced to apply her body, weak and full of pain, to his hands; which he, tying up very rudely and imperfectly, to her exceeding dolour, she complaining of his unskilfulness, his rude handling and the extreme pain he put her to; the duke her grandson being then called and present, and likewise the physician, who much reproving him for the undertaking and performing it so unworthily, was made to leave her, and present commandment was given to seek the king's bone-setter, one called Cuença; who being found after much seeking, came instantly, late at night. He unbinding her arm, exclaimed against the unskilfulness of the former surgeon, felt it splintered,

and so bound it up in the presence of the
physicians, all visiting her together twice or
thrice a day.

Yet this bone-setter's skill proved not so good ;
for she remained still with extremity of pain and
without rest, still complaining that the bone was
not well set. Which a lady, a kinswoman of the
Duke, feeling, wished that a bone-setter out of
the country, whom she had tried, might be sent
for ; commending him much both for his skill
and good fortune in his cures. This man dwelt
twenty-six or twenty-seven leagues from Madrid.
I presently sent for him with the most speed that
might be; who arrived within three days, a plain
country fellow, who would not touch her but in
the presence of the physicians, for which we liked
him the better. He asked her Grace of the manner of her pain, and where it most afflicted her, and
at the coming of the physician he unbound her
arm and palpably showed the error of the cure,
which the physicians plainly saw ; and all present
with the touch of the hand might perceive that a
splint of the cracked bone stood out and was not
fixed in its place. And this was seven or eight
days after the first dressing ; in which time may
be supposed the gre : pain she passed, in so deli-

cate and aged a body of seventy-two years. This man dressed it, bound it up and took upon him the cure; the king's bone-setter being dismissed.

The good duchess remained afterwards from this time forty days together in her bed in one posture, without turning her; for if she stirred, the pain of her arm would force her to lie still on her back; notwithstanding, in these extremities, marvellous was her hope and confidence in Almighty God, passing all with quiet and admirable sufferance and patience, as the holy Tobias. For whereas she had always feared God from her infancy, and kept His commandments, she repined not against God because of the trouble which had befallen her, but continued immovable in the fear of God all the days of her life.[1] In these pains of her arm and breast, and all other adverse chances whatsoever, either corporal or external, she always with a notable conformity submitted herself to the will of our Lord, beseeching His Divine Majesty to do with her as might be most pleasing to His holy service and to the salvation of her soul; and daily, (but chiefly when these pains most troubled and tormented her) did she repeat this sentence in the Spanish

[1] See Tobias ii. 13, 1:.

tongue, written with her own hand in her book of
flowers. "Lord, Thou knowest what is convenient for the health of my soul; I beseech Thee so
to succour my corporal necessities as I may not
lose the spiritual."

The first place of visit that she made going out
of her house after this painful accident, which was
the 26th of· October following, was a pilgrimage
to the chapel of our Blessed Lady at a monastery
of the Dominicans called Atocha, a place of
great concourse and devotion. By which, and
many other troublesome occurrences that came
upon her in this her widow's estate, doth notably
appear the lively trust and Christian hope she
had in God· Almighty, as will likewise be seen in
her last sickness.

I might compare this good duchess in her way
of living to the notablest matrons that have been
in the Christian world. For ordinarily, if possibility of health suffered, she rose with the day in
summer and in winter before day, and being soon
ready, she went into her oratory, where she ·
remained 'until she had heard Mass. For between
seven and eight o'clock in summer-time, but in the
winter somewhat later, her chaplain came to say
Mass; and if both chaplains were at home they

both said Mass, and often other priests and
religious came thither, and ordinarily she heard
all. And having heard Mass she called such
servants as had the guiding of her affairs to know
how business went, and to appoint what should
be done. She daily read the Office of our Blessed
Lady, the Office of the Holy Cross, and of the
Holy Ghost ; at certain times the whole Office of
the Dead, and the Gradual Psalms, and on some
certain special feasts the whole Office of the
Breviary. She no day omitted to say the general
litanies, and other particular litanies as the day
and time required. She weekly, and all the
feasts of the year, frequented the holy Sacraments of Confession and Communion. Never
was she idle, but was either praying, working,
reading or disposing the affairs of her house,
except when strangers or persons of quality came
to visit her, or she in correspondent courtesy
went to visit them ; which time she often complained was burdensome to her. After that her
sight was not so good to work curious works, she
employed her labour to work for the poor ; and
the last she did was to sew and hem sheets for
the hospital. Her other former works were
sumptuous and precious, wrought for God's

service and the use of the Church; and the last she worked were the ornaments for priest and altar given by her to the new English seminary in Madrid.

All the solemn and principal feasts of the year she failed not to hear even-song and High Mass in the monastery of St. Dominic, or of the Angels, being Franciscan nuns in the same street; where the offices were performed with great solemnity, music, and devotion; and she continued there, the whole office being very long. In the Holy Week she was in a manner continually in the church; and the latter four days spent daily there ten or eleven hours.

When her sight failed to see to work, as I say, she passed the most time in reading devout and spiritual books, as the *Meditations of St. Augustine,* his *Confessions,* and the *Manual,* in the Spanish tongue; the lives of Saints, which she daily read herself, being well; and in her weakness they were read to her in the hearing of her women servants. She had ever with this devotion all true humility. She was an enemy to vanity and flattery; yet could not be hidden, as many religious and persons of the best fame desired to be remembered in her prayers, as did that holy nun of St. Francis' Order in Carion de los Condes, whom for rare sanctity and true heavenly virtues, the wisest, learnedest, religiousest, and mightiest in Spain, did admire, whom the king and queen went often to visit and to be partaker of her counsel and prayers. This religious virgin did sometimes write to the duchess, desiring correspondence by letters, some whereof I have seen, and was astonished at the style, to see a woman write with so high wisdom of Divine reasons and counsels of perfection, which to me showed an apostolic spirit. Divers Popes have written particular Briefs to the duchess, commending themselves to her prayers; as Pope Gregory XIII., Pope Sixtus V., Pope Clement VIII., whose letters I have seen and read.[3]

The noble widows of Spain, by a laudable and worthy custom observed among them, are free of the fondness and blemish of affecting worldly fashions; for after the death of their husbands, they retire themselves from all worldly vanity and ostentation, their apparel being the plainest and cheapest stuffs, never wearing gold, silver, jewel, silk or lace. Their own lodgings are

[3] Namely, one of Pope Paul the Fifth, dated at St. Mark's, Rome, 1st May, 1607.

L

hanged in winter with plain, coarse black cloth, and in hotter weather with buckrams, or such coarse poor stuffs. Their servants and attendants had but what was necessary, without show of light bravery. Their own upper garments were worn under a coarse black mantle, a toke of white linen that covers all their person. And seldom or never do they take another husband, except they be heirs, very young and without children. I know a lady, the only daughter of the Marquis of Velada, majordomo mayor to the king, married at eighteen years of age to the Duke of Medina Celi. Before the year came about she had a son and the duke her husband died. She could not be brought to marry again, nor would give her son another father; holding it much dishonour and disparagement to their person, house and children, to marry again. For the law saith: "A woman passing to second vows neglecteth the three best things—God, the memory of her deceased husband, and the love of her children."

Our duchess, when her husband died, was in the thirty-fourth year of her age, mother of one only son, then twelve years old; the duke not above fifty when he died; which, comparing all

their ages together, seemed to be the time that
the delight and comfort of each other should
have been most. She in her husband, not yet
begun to be old; in her son, now growing to
years of understanding; the duke in her, now
married to her thirteen years; now well acquainted with the language, air, customs and
conditions of that country; and the more for
that he was then named and appointed by the
king for governor of the Low-Countries, where
they should have lived so near to England and to
her friends. Herein they both took (as the
duchess told me) an extraordinary consolation;
for the duke, being then with the king, wrote
the Parabien [4] of the news to her, willing her to
advertise her grandmother, who then was alive
at Louvain. But the duchess, although most
glad with the news, wrote again to the duke : "I
dare not write it to my grandmother, lest something might succeed to cross it ; and she, crossed
in the joyful expectation, might turn to the
prejudice of her health and life. And being the
most comfortable news to my temporal desires
which I have heard since my coming out of

[4] Parabien is explained by the dictionary of the Spanish
Academy as meaning Congratulation, Felicitation.

England, yet I dare not believe it, until we be
in the way; lest believing it and not succeeding,
I should do myself no little harm." And these
crosses succeeded that her grandmother died the
same month of July, and the duke in September
following. The son also seemed to be in forward
happiness, being in the age to know the worth of
his father and the goodness and virtue of his
mother. But these delights and comforts were
all wholly dashed with the state of a widow,
who never after took delight in the world but for
the breeding of her son, as was fitting his years
and quality; in all things banishing from herself,
both in clothing and diet, all that might show
deliciousness.

In the year 1588, when that famous hypocrisy
of the Dominican nun of Lisbon, who pretended
the ambition of a Saint, called Soror Maria de
Visitaçion, was discovered ; who by pricking her
head with thorns, by wounding her side and hands
to the imitation of St. Francis and St. Catharine
of Sienna, by putting herself to grievous smart for
this ambitious vanity, would persuade the world
that they were by some sovereign apparition so
fixed in her body as they were in those glorious
Saints, and by counterfeit raptures, had procured

such an esteem as from all parts of Spain they
sent and came to her to have her benediction
and some linen clothes sprinkled with the blood
of her wounds ; which she carried so cunnningly,
as all in a manner held her for a Saint. The
king himself, Philip II., albeit very incredulous in
such matters, but upon firm evidences and testimonies admitted by the Church, yet by sundry
relations made to his majesty began to give credit
to this so general report of the nun. And I have
heard by some, (whether true or no, I know not),
that in the year 1588, when that great Spanish
fleet went for England, many of the banners
were carried to her to bless (a great rashness
and presumption in her to do it), being, as she was,
a mere hyprocrite, shortly after found out and
proved : and after strict examination, being Prior-
ess then of the monastery, confessed by herself
(the same year, the 15th of October) that these
were devices of her invention to be accounted a
Saint. The story is notorious, and had deceived
many wise, great, learned and good Religious.
She, being convicted, was chastised and was very
penitent, refusing no penance, but desiring as
much as flesh and blood might bear.

But to our purpose. While the fame thus ran

of her wounds and of her sanctity, and was generally so reputed, a great Religious man who had seen her and such effects as induced the credit of her supposed sanctity, being with the duchess, she asked some particulars about her, and among the rest of her conversation and diet, whether he knew anything of her in the one and observed her in the other, he being of the same Order. He answered: " Madam, your question is worth the moving, which made me at first to doubt her before I saw the effects, because she converses with most that seek her, especially such as are of reckoning, and spends much time in conversation. For her diet ; she being the Superior in the Convent and held so holy, I know she hath many dainties sent her, and I hear not that she depriveth herself of any part of that which the monastery and the Order allows her." Our Duchess replied. " Is it so ? I fear this sanctity is temporal, and will not long last. For all Saints, memorable to have been great servants of God Almighty, have had their eminence in these two virtues. For their private persons, recollection and abstinence, properly united to the true service of His Divine Majesty, but when necessity and charity enforced. And the contrary (to wit, con-

versation and dainties, with variety of gustful
diet) were baits to worldly love and inducements
to sin ; " alleging the example of St. Martin and
the holy woman that excused herself to see him ;
of St. Francis, St. Dominic, St. Clare and others.

The love of chastity and of chaste persons in
the duchess I have noted before. The least
gesture of the contrary either in shew or speech
was marvellously displeasing to her; she commending very often the pure and clean soul of
Queen Mary her mistress, whose education had
been so chaste and innocent of impurity as she
knew not the meaning of 'sluttish terms or foul,
unchaste words, as I touched in the description
of her life.

I will add here what an ancient lady in England
did tell me of her before my coming to Spain,
who was a courtier. Queen Mary being in the
gallery ready to go to the chapel, within the
traverse, the Lord William Howard,[5] Lord
Chamberlain being with her, he taking his leave ;
without the traverse stood the maids of honour,

[5] Lord William Howard's name occurs very frequently in
the Privy Purse Expenses of the Princess Mary, and in such
terms as to show that he was a frequent visitor in her household.

expecting to wait on the queen to the chapel. Mrs. Frances Neville[6] standing next to the traverse, the Lord Chamberlain passing by, a merry gentleman, took her by the chin, saying: "My pretty . . . .[7] how dost thou?" Which the queen saw and heard, the traverse being drawn. The queen gone forth, finding her farthingale at her foot loose, made sign to Mrs. Neville to pin it, which, kneeling down, she did. The queen then took her by the chin, as he had done saying, "God-a-mercy, my pretty. . . ." She hearing the queen say thus, so blushed as she seemed to be astonished, replying: "Madam, what says your majesty?" still upon her knees, and seemed to be much troubled. The queen answered, "What is the matter? Have I said or done more than the Lord Chamberlain did? And may not I be as bold with thee as he?" She replied: "My Lord Chamberlain is an idle gentleman, and we respect not what he saith or doth; but your majesty, from whom I think never any heard such a word, doth amaze me either in jest or earnest to be called so by you." A . . . is a

---

[6] Possibly the lady who is mentioned in the same Privy Purse Expenses, pp. 192, 196, 197, 198.

[7] The expression here used will not bear repetition.

wicked misliving woman. The queen took it,
"Thou must forgive me; for I meant thee no
harm."

Thus chaste were the thoughts and words
of this renowned princess and such was the
reputation of her family, in which chaste school
was bred this our duchess; excellently well
learning her lesson and imitating her mistress as in her will and purpose she did exceedingly abhor and detest all impurities and
unclean words. And I have known that she
hath plainly, yet with reserved modesty, told
great men of note and worth the dishonour and
misery they purchased to themselves by the base
actions of unchaste lives; and would boldly
reprove such with whom she had any interest of
friendship. Nor were any, of what degree soever,
who had the fame of such a life, ever welcome to
her. And being by chance told that certain
women were met in the duke her grandson's
coach, that had not the best reputation, she
would never afterwards enter again into that
coach. Divers of our noble English gentlemen,
at their being in the court of Spain and visiting
her, admired in her this virtue, so carried with
such a graceful manner as they wished that she

might for a time live in her own country to be
an example of imitation to our great ladies. It
is the virtue that setteth out and adorneth all
other virtues, especially in women, being the
speech of the body and the interpreter of the
mind.

A lie was most odious to her, which in her
pages and younger sort she would have sharply
chastised as an enormous fault.   And the servant
that she found to have told her an untruth fell
much from her favour, she holding it a vice most
unworthy of a Christian.   She, faithful and
punctual in promises, advised before what she
promised, held it a chief point of honour and
religion to perform it.   And for facility in giving
credit to the reports of others, she measured them
by her own intentions, observing this columbine
and candidous simplicity under the rule of charitable construction; albeit in matters that imported the honour of God, the government of her
weightier affairs, her credulity was not so great
and facile, but directed by the rule of God's
Church and discussed with that prudence as she
would not easily be deceived or over-reached.

Of mildness had she great use at her first
coming into Spain, particularly among the kin-

dred of the duke her husband, his mother then living; who was not pleased with the match, for that she had purposed to marry the duke with her grandchild, the daughter of Count Don Pedro, her eldest son. But the duke, avoiding and preventing so near a match in blood as his niece, married as he did; which so angered his mother as she married her to his younger brother (as hath been said) and passed to him the Marquisship of Pliego, an estate of one hundred thousand ducats by the year, and so made a suit between the two brothers. Yet the duchess carried herself towards her mother-in-law, with that mildness and affable respect as it afterwards grieved the Marquesa of what she had done; and she continued to the children of the younger brother (whereof I am a witness) that love and regard as if her husband had suffered no wrong by their father, and the like to all the kindred; notwithstanding the suit was on foot between her son and his cousin-german, the heir of that house; so gracious and mild was she in forgetting injuries.

CHAPTER XIII.

I HAVE before showed the bringing up of her son
and the pious government of her house, family
and children; yet I may not omit a discreet
policy that she used in the education of the
dukes, her son and grandson, to make them follow
their book and apply their lessons.

Their first exercise in the morning was to hear
Mass, which was done before eight o'clock. Then
they went to their book, their master being in the
house, he read them their lesson; which heard
and they able to construe, they broke their fast.
Then were they set a task, which they were to
repeat to their master before dinner. When dinner was ready and to be brought in, she asked
their master if they had done their lessons. If

yea, all well; and there was some reward, or contentment, commending their diligence; if no, the
duchess commanded presently not to bring in the
meat, telling them with a sweet reprehension,
" Although you will not dine yourselves; yet keep
not me from my dinner at a due time; for I must
not nor can eat until you have done your lessons
and said your book as you ought; and so I, your
mother, (when he learned, to her son; and to her
grandson, I your grandmother) an old woman,
must be punished for your negligence. You see my
care is that you want nothing that is fit for you,
and I must want my meat for your play and idleness. Go to your study and make an end quickly
that the meat be not spoiled, for we must all fast
till you have done." Which served as a prudent
correction and discreet encouragement to them to
apply to their books, and diligently to perform
their studies in due time.

I showed before the singular zeal this lady and
the duke her husband used in the time of Lent,
and especially in the Holy Week, and the great
feasts of the year, with marvellous devotion, humility and charity to the poor Descalços Friars
De La Lapa, in serving them and feeding them.
And it is very ordinary among the great ladies in

Spain to visit hospitals and to give the sick and diseased to eat with their own hand, to serve them, to wipe their sores, to cleanse their wounds, to feed and cherish them with such alacrity and humble diligence as evidently sheweth that it proceedeth from true fervour of Christian devotion and piety, which is really to wash the feet of saints.

The Cardinal of Rhemes calleth our duchess another Queen Helena, who with liberal bounty employed her goods to succour the Scots, English and Irish, and other afflicted and fugitive Catholics, who had recourse into Spain for the exercise of their faith and religion. At one time she procured the release of thirty-eight Englishmen, prisoners in Seville, being all taken in the West Indies and sentenced to die, and some merchants accused for assisting them with shipping and other provision for that voyage. As one Mr. Norris, a merchant of Barnstaple in Devonshire, and sometime Mayor of that town, and one of that company, hath told me, much magnifying the charity and affection of the duchess to her distressed countrymen, and the obligation that he and his followers had to her for their lives and liberty. At divers other times, especially after the differences grew to professed quarrels between the crowns of England and Spain, sundry such adverse accidents falling out, men having recourse to our duchess, by her mediation had their release procured and their present extremities assisted with liberal benevolence, although I hold few of these for saints; yet because they fell into trouble, she of her goodness was forward to help them; which I think Sir Richard Hawkins of Plymouth, prisoner in Madrid in the latter time of Queen Elizabeth, will acknowledge.

But to come to a saint, (one who at least died a saint and martyr) when the Queen of Scots, forced by her rebellious subjects to leave her country, had fled into England, expecting there to have refuge and assistance, according to promise, found the contrary, to wit, restraint and such other hard measure as her rents out of France came not to her; which our good duchess understanding, solicited the duke her husband, then living, in her behalf, who sent her twenty thousand ducats to relieve her present necessities.

If acts of charity to Catholic priests and gentlemen of our country, whom domestic calamities and oppressions caused to seek refuge abroad, should be here particularly set down, I should enter into a large narration, and could myself declare many particulars, the bounty of which pious actions has passed to many by my hands. But in so doing I should do wrong to the godly intention of the good lady, although deceased, who could not endure to have such deeds numbered nor yet remembered, who not willingly would have their own names, or the names of their friends, mentioned in this kind. This our good duchess had spared much from the lustre of herself, both for diet (in which she was marvellous temperate) and for other appurtenances to her person, to be able to do the more good works.

It hath fallen out in the time that I served her often, and was her usual custom, when any gentleman of quality that she knew and had any acquaintance with her, that lay sick and was thought to be in want, she commanded her steward, or the gentleman that had the charge of the private expenses of her house, to put up (tied in a paper) a hundred crowns, or sixty, or or fifty, or forty, or thirty, or twenty, or so much as it pleased her, according to the want and condition of the party, which she would take so

bound up, and put in her pocket when she went to
visit the party; and after salutation and pious advices as occasion was offered, at her coming away,
taking leave with words of comfort, would put the
paper under the pillow of the sick person. And
to others with whom she was not so well acquainted in their distress, if any spake to our duchess for
them, she seldom or never denied, but they tasted
her bounty according to their quality and her
means. She was very respective and compassionate to such as were of noble blood and
ingenuous education, who by some disaster had
fallen into wants; pitying their estate that had
been fed and bred with plenty and were afterward
necessitated to have relief and sustenance by the
alms and bounty of strangers. Of this sort, of
our country, of Irish and of Spaniards and
French also, I could relate them that in a high
kind were beholding to the bounty of our duchess.

Her ordinary allowance was to give bread and
money to the poor religious monasteries and
hospitals of Madrid, and to those of St. Francis
bread and eggs. An ordinary allowance of alms
every month was to be given in money by the
gentlewoman that kept the expenses of the house
to such poor as asked at the door. Never any

M

English priest or other stranger, poor Englishman
or other that pretended need, who asked of her,
or otherwise by some of her servants .desired
relief of their wants, but had from her a charitable benevolence. And seldom did she refuse
to see any Englishman who asked it, were he
never so mean. The general hospital of Madrid,
weekly, as is said, received her alms, and in
other necessities were succoured with sheets and
blankets required. Many poor widows and
orphans in the duke's estate had perpetual
maintenance by her charity. Many Sundays and
Holy-days did she send the whole supper of the
Recollects Descalços of St. Francis's Order in
Madrid with some extraordinary good supply,
being particularly devoted to that Order. For
she herself had taken the habit of the Third
Order of St. Francis and was professed in it,
wearing under her outward garment the habit
and scapulary while she lived. In suits or
pretences that any of our countrymen had in the
court of Spain, very forward was she, if they
sought it, with her best means to assist them, to
write in their favour to the Lords of the Council,
and to send some friend or servant with them to
further their business. And such as wanted

found other aidful relief. Thus was she daily in doing good works.

If her means had answered her desires for the founding, furnishing and adorning of monasteries, she had been one of the notablest patronesses in the Christian world, wholly addicted to the service of God and the glorifying of His eternal Name. I have heard our duchess say that if in her time, our kingdom should be so happy as to admit the public face of Catholic Religion again, she would endeavour to be the first with the poor means she had to build a monastery of St. Francis's Order and completely to furnish it; knowing and acknowledging the general good that those Religious do in a christian country; and while she lived she built the monastery of Monte-Virgine of that Order, Descalços Recollects, and Santa Marina in Zafra, Nuns of the Order of St. Clare. Through the whole course of her life she was not sparing in advancing these good works; as in repairing St. Onophrio de la Lapa, our Lady del Rosario of St. Dominic; in furnishing these and others with rich ornaments, costly pictures; devout confraternities; as all the churches and monasteries in Zafra and all in the duke's estate have her in perpetual memory.

Also she procuring from the Apostolic See great privileges and indulgences for their better establishing, continuance and increase; the effect whereof the great church of Zafra and Sta. Clara, an ancient rich monastery of Franciscan Nuns in that town, do largely enjoy. Fray Juan Baptista Moles saith (in his book and chapter before alleged), "There are two hermitages, one very ancient and dedicated to St. Onophrio and St. Paul the first hermit; and the other, which the duchess, the Lady Jane Dormer, built to St. John the Evangelist, very beautiful, pleasant and devout, which Don Juan de Ribera, Bishop of Badajos, and afterwards Archbishop of Valencia and Patriarch of Antioch, did consecrate." And our duchess, in the end of her life, all that she could leave besides her household stuff which descended to the duke, and some few remembrances left to friends and servants (for there was no servant that served her, at the time of her death, but had some remembrance or legacy given him) and besides what was bequeathed to the poor and to say Masses for her soul, all was left to monasteries. Yea, the annuities that she left for life to her most obliged servants were in reversion to the cloister of Santa Marina, in which she had

built a marvellous fair church with a fair gallery
from the duke's palace ; and above, at the end of
the gallery, an oratory, from which they may hear
and see Mass at the high altar, in which work is
showed magnificence and devotion.

CHAPTER XIV.

OF THE SICKNESS AND LAST DAYS OF THE DUCHESS OF FERIA.

AFTER the breaking of her arm, the extreme pain
of her breast still continuing, our duchess daily
grew weaker, and many times with such accidents
of hot agues as in that great age and feebleness
of body she was ordered by the physicians to be
let blood. So finding herself with a perpetual
decay of strength and health she only expected
that which escapes none ; having in her memory
and often repeating that of the wise man, "*Me-
morare novissima tua, et in æternum non peccabis.*"
To this end she had fastened to her beads a
death's-head (which beads she put into my hand,
dying ; which I have and much esteem), on which

she meditated and often discoursed, having learnt of St. Hierome that notable sentence: "He easily contemns all things, whose thoughts always tell him that he must die." And also for this end, she had made her testament and disposed her estate, having (as is shewed before) taken the habit of penance of the Third Order of St. Francis, to be participant of the graces and indulgences of that holy religion. She had entered herself into the list and number *de Ancillis,* or handmaids of our Blessed Lady, when in Sta. Ursula at Alcala, a convent of Franciscan nuns, was founded a sisterhood or congregation of them with this title, "to the Queen of Angels;" rejoicing to be the *Ancilla* of her, by whose mediation and gracious intercession she might attain grace to die well. Likewise did she ordain, many months before her death, her coffin to be made, in which her body should be entered, which when ordered, and the measure to be taken of her body, her women grew tender and wept, the duchess said: "Why weep you? For this must be, and it cannot be long before it come—Weep not, but pray for me. We must all die; but that which imports, is to die well and to have a good end. And this is that which I request of you all to commend me

to God, that He vouchsafe to give me His grace
to end well."

Our duchess kept her bed almost twelve months
before her death, pained through her whole body,
especially in her arm that had been broken; for
although it had been set and cured, yet the pain
of her breast kept it very weak. And once,
taking her little grand-daughter in her arms,
being then the only child of the duke her grandson, when the nurse took it from her, it so
chanced as her arm a little strained, put her to
that extremity of pain as she was falling down
in a swoon; and after that it put her to such
trouble and affliction as she could not lift it to
her head, nor pluck out a pin with that hand, but
carried it always in a scarf. Notwithstanding
this infirmity and other exceeding dolours of her
body, the same still was the exercise of her
Christian virtues and her zeal to God's service;
for weekly she both confessed and communicated,
had daily good men with her; no day did she
leave to hear Mass. For when her weakness
began to be such as she could hardly remain out
of her bed, by license of the vicar of the Archbishop of Toledo, (who himself came to see the
place for the decency of it,) her oratory was

removed to another part, as from her bed, through the passage that entered into her chamber, she might see the altar, hear Mass, behold and adore the holy Sacrifice, which was her true comfort ; and so enjoyed it to the time of her decease, for the day that she died she heard Mass. Before her oratory was thus changed, in the summer-time she lay in a bedstead that turned with wheels, which at the time of Mass was set before the door of the oratory. But when winter came she was forced to remove to a warmer chamber; and had her oratory altered, as is said before.

In the same time of this her sickness that Father Ribadeneira, (a very reverend, wise, learned and ancient Father of the Society; for he had lived seventy-one years in the Order, much respected and reverenced by the duchess, who likewise answered her grace with the same good-will and regardful affection,) whom I mentioned before, having known her in England ; she, in all important occasions advised with him, asked his counsel, he esteeming her a very true and able friend, and often visiting her as to whose favours, both in his own particular and for the benefit of his Order, he stood much beholding.

He dedicated to her (as before is noted [1]) his book
De los santos Estravagantes; to wit, such as were
not in the Roman calendars of breviaries and
missals.   It fell out, I say, that this good Father,
in September, 1610, fell mortally sick; she then
also lying in her bed sick.   This, among other
afflictions, she accounted not the least, to want
the assistance of so dear and esteemed a Father;
and sent often to visit him, myself being for the
most part the messenger.   And the last message
he sent her was this : " Commend me much to
the duchess, and tell her that shortly we shall
see each other in Paradise."   This message she
would have me repeat to her more than once,
and took in it extraordinary consolation.   This
holy Father departed this world (I was present
when he died) the 22nd of September, in the
eighty-fifth year of his age, after great labours
and travels taken in his religion, many worthy
works set out by him to the edification of the
Christian world, as appeareth in the catalogue of
the writers of the Society, printed at Antwerp.[2]

[1] See p. 7.

[2] See *Catalogus Scriptorum religionis Societatıs Jesu, auctore P.
Petro Ribadeneira,* p. 225—229, ed. Antv. 1613, 8vo.   It is stated
in his epitaph that he died at Madrid, 22nd September, 1611.
Also *Histoire du Père Ribadeneyra,* par le Père J. M. Prat. Paris,
1862.

It pleased Almighty God, at that time also, to take out of this world the most virtuous and good Queen of Spain, who died at St. Laurence by the Escurial, the 3rd of October, 1611.[8] Which when our duchess heard, condoling the great loss of the whole kingdom; (for her majesty was not twenty-eight years complete), having so many princely children deprived of so good a mother in the flower of her age; commanding presently mourning to be made for her servants, saying: " All Spain and Germany had true cause to mourn; but she was worthy of a better kingdom, which this good lady had attained in so young years; and I, poor woman and decrepit, do languish in this bed with pain and misery." Our duchess sent me to give the *Pesumè* to the queen's ghostly Father, a Jesuit, that came with her out of Germany, condoling his and the general loss. In doing the message, he could not for tears answer me, but wept like a child.

In this extreme sickness, the pains being extraordinary that our good duchess suffered, yet when any came to visit her, were he religious, or a neighbour, or any gentlemam of our country, she received him with that alacrity and cheerfulness

---

[8] This was Margaret of Austria, wife of Philip III., King of Spain, and daughter of Charles, Archduke of Gratz.

of countenance, as increased an affectionate
respect from them to her. Yea, such was the
sweetness of her condition as drew a certain
reverence and esteem from them who conversed
with her; and in this conversation, such was her
mildness, gravity, and gracious deportment, as
after such visit they affected and honoured her
much more, as well might be applied to her what
the Holy Scripture saith of the noble and
memorable widow Judith : "And she was among
all most famous, because she feared our Lord
very much; neither was there that spake an ill
word of her." [4]   In this sickness, marvellous was
the care our duchess took and the strict account
to make full satisfaction where any thing might
be due, not alone for matters past but for to
come, and so she had provided for the burial;
and the exact accomplishment of her testament,
having committed the charge to her faithful
servants. For the better clearing of all questions,
she wrote, some months before she died, to the
Contador and Treasurer, officers of the duke's
estate, (whereof she had been governess many
years, as hath been said) charging them before
God, that if they knew or could understand any

[4] See Judith, viii. 8.

thing wherein she might be indebted by way of justice or conscience that they should advise her; commanding them to take pains and use diligence to search and inquire if there should be any cause for restitution, and to demand and hear the complaints of all, and to advertise her that they might be remedied. These letters I wrote. And likewise did she call a servant, whom she much trusted, under whose charge passed, some years before she died, the general and great receipts and expenses of all accounts in her house, to have great care of this particular for satisfaction, commanding him to look well about and remember her where she might have any obligation. So Christian and fervent was her desire completely to satisfy with all that might be due in justice or conscience. And to her great cost did she deal with some, more by the way of pitiful than of obliged. As but three days before she died, taking compassion upon the master carpenter that had taken, too great, all the timber-work of the church of Sta. Marina, complaining that he had overshot himself in the bargain and was too great a loser, desired by way of petition to be considered. She did, having examined the business, in compassionate favour grant his suit and signed the Libranças for the recovery of this money; which the man took so gratefully when I gave him the Libranças (or warrants), wishing him to give some alms to the poor monastery in gratuity, he promised at the receipt of the money to give them a hundred ducats. Until three days before our duchess died she omitted not the saying of her usual prayers, as the Office of our Blessed Lady, her beads, and to have read to her the life of the Saint of the day. When she had not possibility of health to read her Office herself, she willed some other to read it for her.

On Thursday night, the 19th of January, her infirmity increasing, I was present while her excellency supped, which she seemed to eat with appetite and reasonable gust, her supper being a partridge and some jelly. After grace was said, she remaining sitting up in her bed, to wash her mouth and hands, as she usually did, she shewed so strangely fair with colour in her face, so clear and lively, as those who were present stood and admired at her sudden beauty; so as one said to another, "Did you ever see a fairer face? What may be the cause of this alteration? Is her grace turned young again?" And an ancient gentlewoman in the company (I was present) was bold to say to her, "Madam, your grace looks strangely fair on the sudden." She only smiled but replied nothing. One[5] of her servants that understood somewhat of the nature of the pulse, and in the absence of the physicians her grace did usually command him to take hers, a little before she went to take rest that night, taking it, told her women at his going out of the chamber, that my lady was not well, her pulse showed a greater weakness ; and that he perceived a certain malicious increase of her ague. And therefore on Friday morning very early he came to see how she had passed that night, and what had succeeded. Then he found her pulse much worse and her forces strangely weakened. Her grace asked him how he liked her pulse ? He answered with leisure, not so well as he wished. She importuned him to know the whole particular, and charged him to tell her plainly and truly his opinion. He told her the truth, and what he thought. And she acknowledged that in the same manner, or rather worse, she herself felt that her spirits were much debilitated, and

[5] In the margin of the original MS. this is said to have been " the author " himself.

it was pain to her to speak. When, not long
after, the physicians came to visit her, they confessed they found her much altered since the
day before ; yet gave her comfort that there was
not so great danger as she imagined. As her
weakness they said was more, so they appointed
her to drink goat's milk, fresh drawn. But perceiving these to be but delays and dilatory
medicines of doctors, feeling herself in danger,
although she yielded to what they prescribed,
having a thirsty desire to be with God, she commanded and ceased not to call upon us, until
order was given to bring her from the parish
church the Blessed Sacrament, *pro Viatico*,
albeit she had communicated but three or four
days before. This the physicians, under pretence
not to disanimate her, would have deferred,
alleging the present necessity not to be so great ;
until by more importunity of her grace, It was
brought to her on Saturday night, at nine o'clock,
which she received with marvellous gust and
devotion, answering with good memory and
zealous promptitude to all questions that are
demanded when in such case the Blessed Sacrament is administered.

In this occasion, the duke, her grandson, came

to ask her blessing upon his knees, and forgiveness of all displeasures and offences, offering
himself, his service, and his goods, to accomplish
all that her excellency should order and command; and with this grew tender. She took this
offer with an affectionate impression, although
she intended to charge him with nothing, only
commended to him her servants and gave him
her blessing with much goodwill and love of a
mother, adding some short lessons of good
counsel.

That night she passed resting very little,
spending most of the time in prayer and hearken-
ing to the Religious men that were about her;
for almost continually from this evening to her
decease there were with her two Fathers of the
Society, four Franciscan friars, one Dominican
Father, her chaplain, and myself.

On Sunday, the extremity increasing, she
desired with great instance the Sacrament of
Extreme Unction, which was brought and given
her at ten o'clock in the forenoon; which likewise
she received with great devotion and demonstra-
tion of her Christianity. And with others that
were present when they gave her this Sacrament,
was Don Juan Idiaques, an ancient councillor of

Estate, President of the Council of Orders and generally of great name and respect in Spain, who after that she had received the Sacrament, went to her bedside to kiss her hands and to take his last leave. To him standing upon his knees, (for he would not be entreated to stand otherwise) she made a speech; with so good words and reasons commending to his favour and protection, her house and the duke her grandson, as the President remained as it were amazed to see so great weakness and together such an understanding and memory in her affairs. He shedding many tears on going out of her chamber, said to us, " It is a thing to praise God for, to see this lady how well she stands with God, and the spirit that she hath."

After her grace had received this Sacrament, her servants came to her chamber to ask forgiveness and to take her blessing. There was nothing seen nor heard but tears and sighs. To all did she give pardon with gracious countenance and very good will, willing them all to pray for her. Likewise most of the great ladies that were in Madrid came to take their last leave and ask her blessing. Such was the reverence of her age, the example of her life and regard of her virtue.

N

The same afternoon an English knight, a
kinsman of our duchess, Sir Robert Chamberlain,[6]
came also to take his leave; a chief motive of his
coming to Madrid, as he said, was to kiss her
hand. He now sorry to see her in that plight,
so near her end, beseeched her blessing, and to
command him something in her service. She
said to him: "Cousin, you see my speech begins
to fail me; but what I wish you is, that you look
to it, to stand strong and firm in the Catholic
Faith. I know well that Catholics suffer great
troubles in England; but take care you lose not
the goods of heaven for the goods of the earth.
And so God Almighty bless you and keep you;"
commanding after a jewel to be given him of
one hundred ducats, which, after her death, I
bought and gave him.

That night between eight and nine o'clock she
had a trance, so extreme and violent that we all
thought it would have ended her. And while she
was in the combat of this fit, not altogether losing
her sense, the Religious about her called to her to

---

[6] A letter from Sir John Digby to the Earl of Salisbury,
from Madrid, dated 19th January, 1612, st. vet. mentions the
arrival there of Sir Robert Chamberlain, and the death of the
duchess on the night of Monday, 13th January.

name Jesus; if she could not with her tongue, yet with her mind to call upon Him and to trust in His Sacred Passion, putting in her hand a little crucifix which she often kissed, embraced it ; and when she recovered her speech repeated verbatim the words that the Fathers had said to her, and of herself (only with perfect memory) the whole hymn, *O Gloriosa Domina, Excelsa super sidera,* etc.; and many times repeated

> Maria, Mater gratiæ,
> Mater misericordiæ ;
> Tu nos ab hoste protege,
> Et hora mortis suscipe.
> Crux Christi, protege nos ;
> Crux Christi, salva nos ;
> Crux Christi, defende nos.

And in a manner her speech was always : " Jesu, Maria, be with me; Mother of God, help me; good Jesu, deliver me from these troubles." And in this sort, taking at times a little broth of substance passed to the next morning; excusing herself to the Religious that had taken such pains with her that night. And in this interim, that night she spake promptly and readily of divers things with the servant[7] whom she trusted, com-

[7] Most probably the author himself.

mending to his charge certain alms of much charity to divers persons.

This day, Monday, being the last day of her life in this world, and in Spain a holiday of St. Hildefonsus, Bishop of Toledo, which at midnight she had mind of; for such was then her memory, as knowing it to be passed twelve o'clock, she said to me: "This is now St. Hildefonsus's day; to-morrow, Tuesday, our Blessed Lady of Peace (for so it is observed in the archbishopric of Toledo); Wednesday, St. Paul's day; and Thursday, the 26th of January, St. Polycarpus's day, the day that my son died in Naples." This day, I say, being holiday, she called and took care all her people should hear Mass. And when she saw the priest vested, she asked me, if all her women were there? Which Mass, notwithstanding being so weak and lying in her bed, she attended and heard with great devotion. About twelve o'clock the same day, a paroxysm or trance came upon her, so violent as she seemed to be wholly without sense and breathing to the last of her life; so as we all held her for departed; until, after a little space, they named, with a loud voice, the Name of Jesus, she a little bowed down her head without any other motion, and continued in this trance very near an hour.

When she was come to herself and had taken a little broth, the young duchess, her daughter-in-law, told her that the Lady Digby, wife of the English Lord Ambassador, had been there to see her grace, but finding her in that agony was returned home. Her grace answered, " I would I had seen her." The duchess presently with haste sent her coach for her, sending her word that her grace was yet alive, and if she would come, might see her. The lady came as soon as she heard it, with all possible expedition. And coming into our duchess' chamber, drew near to the bedside, other company that were there giving her place. It seemed by her grace's countenance that she was glad of her coming; and after salutations, the one bidding welcome, the other condoling to see her so sick, our duchess said to her these words: "Lady, I speak with much difficulty; and that which I have not strength to say I refer to this Father; " for there stood at her bed's head, Father Creswell, an English Father of the Society.[8] " Your Lady-

---

[8] Father Joseph Creswell, S.J. See De Backer, 1—1464, Oliver, 1—78.

ship is now come into a country and place of
Catholics where you may see and learn ; and if you
do not, the fault is yours.   And believe me, Lady,
and I do tell it you, dying, *That there is no salvation
out of the Catholic Roman Church ;* nor true faith
but that which Catholics profess.   And if your
ladyship desires to save your soul, look to this
which imports you."   The Lady Digby answered :
" Madame, I desire nothing so much, as reason
is I should, as the salvation of my soul ; and I
trust that the Lord will have mercy upon me ;
for in the law and religion wherein I have been
bred, I desire to serve Him."   Her grace replied :
" Lady, desires are not enough, it is necessary to
put it into work, and no work is good but that
which is by the faith and teaching of the Church.
I lack strength to speak more ; look well to it ;
this is it which most imports you."   And so bade
her farewell ; the Lady Ambassador weeping
very much to see our Duchess draw so near to
her end.

When the Lady Digby was gone, one that stood
on the further side of the bed, which was towards the wall, asked her Grace [9] how she did,

---

[9] Here again we recognise the writer of this narrative, and
in the incident recorded a few lines afterwards.

and where she had been an hour since (meaning
when she was in that great trance), telling her
that we all thought she had been in heaven.
She answered: "Surely, I was very near, why
did they call me back again?" Which was no
small comfort to me and all that heard it. An
hour after, she turned again into another trance,
but not so violent as was the last; for she had her
sense and always showed signs of devotion when
they named Jesus or Maria, with bowing down
her head and opening her eyes towards heaven.
After a little time, her speech returning again,
the same party came to her Grace, offering his
service in what she pleased to command, and
withal asked what she would have? She answered in English. "Health (pausing a little,
added) in heaven, which I hope will quickly
come; for we are in the Vespers of our Lady of
Peace,[10] who in peace will receive my soul this
night. Jesus, Maria, be with me. Sweet Jesus,
have mercy on me."

A little time after, they brought to her the two
young grandchildren, the daughters of the duke,

[10] A marginal note here tells us that on "the twenty-fourth
of January, in the diocese of Toledo, is celebrated the feast of
our Lady of Peace."

her grandson.   She gave them her ‚blessing, asking it from heaven for them and for herself, which
was not far off; for then, her spirits beginning to
fail, within a matter of two hours after (that time
being spent by the Religious about her in godly
exhortations, prayers, and Divine service used in
such occasions), a little after nine o clock in the
night on the 23rd of January, 1612, sweetly without any trouble more than the pangs of death,
which were very short, she rendered her blessed
soul to God for to live with Him eternally.

CHAPTER XV.

THUS, our virtuous duchess left this transitory world to receive the reward of her virtue with the Saints of God, whereof we may have more than probable or moral hope that she was soon made partaker, considering what passed in the foresaid trances. She had suffered many months of purgatory in this world; led a laudable and exemplary christian life; and ended it with much edification and consolation of all the assistants; for when her tongue failed, which was some half-hour before she deceased, her hands and eyes showed her faith and desire to be with God. And the last temporal thing that she spoke when her speech began to fail her was to her maid who attended at her bed's feet, bidding her to put in decency and handsomely her bed-clothes about her body, to the end, no doubt, she might die with seemly decency so as to prevent what perhaps the pangs of death might cause.

So this our duchess, on the octave of her birth (for she was born on the sixth of February), did return her happy soul to her Creator to attain the sum of her felicity; and left her body remaining, with the face so beautiful, her hands so fair and flexible, wonderful in that great age, that they seemed rather of a heavenly creature than of a dead body. So dressed up in a poor Franciscan habit, which she had kept by her many years for that purpose to be her outward shroud (which had been the cast garment of a holy good Friar) and with a scapular of St. Dominic's Order, she was laid thus upon a pallet with her face uncovered and her hands held up close together, as the use is to hold them praying.

In the meantime the duke, her grandson, being there, the Teniente of the town was called, (who is the judge in civil causes) and the scrivener that had written and sealed up her testament, to unseal it, open it, and read it publicly before the said Teniente, the duke, and others appointed. For so had our duchess ordained, that as soon as she should be departed this world, the duke (if

he were in the town) should be present at the
reading of her testament to ratify it if he pleased
or otherwise, if he should take any exceptions
about any legacies, to shew the cause before the
Justice. When the Teniente was come before
the duke, the Marquis de Malpica, the Conde de
los Arcos, Don Alonso de Cordova, Don Francisco
Garnica and others, where I was also present,
the testament was opened and read aloud by the
scrivener; which all heard with attention, the
reading of it continuing about an hour. Which
when read, the Teniente asked the duke if his
excellency would ratify and confirm it? He
answered, "Most willingly," and then subsigned
it with his hand. The Teniente, also signing it,
said, "I see no other defect in this testament but
one, that it is not printed, that others might learn
by it to make their testament; because I see in
it the lively points and effects of great charity,
rare wisdom, worthy virtue and true Christian
zeal." This said the judge of the town of Madrid.
The conclusion of which testament I will add
here, being directed to the duke her grandson,
her heir, as her last blessing, translated out of
the Spanish, which is as follows, *verbatim* :—

"After having commended my soul to our

Lord, for the love and most intimate affection I
bear to the duke, Don Gomez, as my grandchild,
and lord of the house of his father, I require and
beseech and charge him, that he take for foundation of all his actions the holy fear of our Lord
God; having care to give no place in his soul to
sin, nor to differ one point from the observance
of God's commandments.   Be, my son, very
charitable and an almsgiver; have about thee
honest and virtuous company; take counsel of
persons well-intentioned and virtuous; exercise
thyself in the acts of a Christian gentleman as
thy ancestors have done; govern thy vassals with
the love of a father and amorous lord; take compassion of the poor, favour the good, repress the
wicked and do justice with equality; procuring
to root out of thy estate public sins and offences
of our Lord, Whom I humbly beseech, by the
merits of His most holy Passion and of His
most holy Mother our Blessed Lady, and St.
Francis and St. Dominic, that He bless thee, and
with His blessing give thee His Divine grace and
those excellent favours which He accustometh to
give to His elect; that I, thy grandmother, and
in love more than any, as much as I can, in the
Name of the most holy Trinity, do bless thee

within and without; and conformable to this His holy blessing do again beseech Him that He obtain for thee and thy successors that which may be to the glory of the same God and good of thy soul and body, and goods and vassals. Amen. I pray thee that thou have me in thy memory, to command to say Masses for my soul, and for the souls of the duke thy father, and of the duke my lord, thy grandfather, who are in rest."

When the testament was read, signed and ratified by the justice and by the duke, order was presently taken that night to accomplish with the soonest expedition, what the testament commanded; which was principally to say Masses for her soul. For she had ordained, as soon as might be after her departure, a hundred Masses should be said in the privileged altars of the town of Madrid; and there also ordered to be sung twenty-four Masses of Requiem. In the state of Feria she had ordained to be said three thousand Masses, besides the sung Masses for nine days together, after her burial; good allowance given for all these Masses. She had bequeathed very liberally to the poor of Madrid, and to the poor monasteries there, to pray for her soul. She gave two hundred ducats to the poor of the town of *Zaphra*, and a very charitable benevolence to the monasteries there; ordering that twelve poor men should be thoroughly clothed to accompany her body at the burial, and to each of them twelve reals in money. Also she remembered with good alms our English Carthusians. No man-servant of hers but had mourning, a hat, a cassock and coat of good cloth; and the women theirs as was fit; and every one some good remembrance according to their quality and merit.

The next morning her body was put into the coffin, wrapped in lead, because it was to be carried to *Zaphra* to the monastery of Sta. Clara, there to be put in the vault under the high choir, among the other coffins of the lords of that house. She willed in her testament to be laid by the duke her husband; saying that loving together so well in life, it was meet their bodies should not be parted in death. *Zaphra* is some two-hundred English miles from Madrid, where she died. That night before she was chested, divers came to see the sweetness and fairness of that face, kissing her hands upon their knees, imagining she was in place to pray for them.

The coffin was set up high in the greater room of the house, set round with torches and wax lights, above and beneath, covered with a hearse-cloth of new black velvet, which the young duchess sent; so large, as the tomb standing higher than a man's head, it lay spread on both the ends and sides upon the ground. In the same room were set up two altars, where continually from six o'clock to twelve, Masses were said and Responsories by divers Religious. And in the afternoon many came and prayed at the hearse.

The day following, at three o'clock in the morning, the body was put in a coach to be carried to Zaphra, attended by her own servants and twelve of the duke's (whereof his secretary was one), her chaplain and an Augustine Friar; for she had expressly commanded by her will to be carried with the least pomp and the most secret. This journey, which was nine days in travel, (for we entered in Zaphra on the second of February) was with the fairest weather, and as pleasant a voyage as could be wished, although we passed the great high mountains that part Castille from Estramadura, (where ordinarily is tempest and bitter storms in the winter; for in

our return we had sharp cold winds, hail and
snow) and being in the end of the month of
January, which is not a season so settled for fair
and warm weather.   And withal such a conformity and good agreement in all the company,
(albeit there were pages, under-servants and
hired fellows that served the coaches and mules,
which usually are not the most orderly), as every-
one did his duty; no murmuring, no grudging,
no complaining, nor the least disgust in the
world.   Which I really have reason to attribute
to the body of our good duchess that we carried.
For divers times the same winter before she died,
in November and December, the weather being
very cold, rainy and tempestuous, she did say to
me and others: "If I should die now, what
trouble should I give my servants to carry my
body?"   But then did we reply: "Fear not; she
that gave not trouble in life, will not give it in
death;" which was, as I may say, miraculously
fulfilled. And when we drew near to our journey's
end, entering into the precincts of the town of
Zaphra, it began to rain so as the whole town
cried: "The blessing of God is come;" for they
wanted rain exceedingly and had prayed long for
it; and that night they had enough, so that all

which were on horseback were thoroughly wet, and we that were in coaches were not wholly dry.

Upon Candlemas day, between five and six o'clock in the evening, we entered into *Zaphra*. Out of the town, the magistrates, gentlemen and chiefest inhabitants did meet the body with torch-light, and so accompanied it to the church of Sta. Marina, which church our duchess had built, and where lay buried the body of her cousin, Mrs. Margaret Harrington, the Lord Harrington's sister; where was erected a goodly monument in the middle of the church to place the body upon. The nuns did sing Vespers and a nocturn *de Defunctis*; which done, all the company were disposed to their lodgings in several principal men's houses, who entertained us extraordinary well.

The next morning the magistrates and we that brought the body met together at the Contador's house, who governed the estate, and with him as chief mourner went to the church, where was sung a solemn Mass and a sermon preached by a Franciscan Friar, much in praise of our duchess. In the afternoon the body was to be carried to Sta. Clara, where it was to be interred, which was done in this solemn manner. Most of the religious of all Orders in the whole estate

were present with their crosses. The Priests of
the town in their surplices and copes; the Dean
of the High Church doing the Office, having a
very rich cope of black velvet richly embroidered
with gold and the dalmatics of the deacon and
the sub-deacon answerable. These the duke her
son had caused to be made in Sicily, with the
antependiums and furniture for six altars; for so
many are in the Church of Sta. Clara; and they
are the fairest and richest ornaments to be used
pro defunctis that I have seen in Spain, or else-
where; and the first time that they were used, it
was for the duke that caused them to be made.
And albeit the way was not long between the two
monasteries, yet they made three stations, singing
a Responsory, with a prayer and incensing, certain low pillars being set, covered with black
cloth to set the body upon.

Being entered into Sta. Clara, the body was
placed on a stately high monument in the high
choir; and the nuns sung vespers and the noc-
turns of requiem. The same night, shewing to
the Abbess of Sta. Clara, who then was Donna
Maria de Mendoça, a niece of the duke of
Infantadgo, what was to be performed by the
testament of the duchess, whose will was that

her body should be there interred with the bodies
of the dukes, her husband and son; and that the
abbess, before a public notary, should accept the
conditions for accomplishing the anniversaries
and other rites ordered by the testament. The
abbess and other of the nuns answered, they
would first see whether the body were there.
For, say they, we see a coffin, but we must see
that the body is in it. Which whether it was
necessary to open the coffin being so locked, and
the body in lead, and the long time that it had
rested there would be troublesome; or that the
abbess suspected the body might be taken out, it
was questioned. For the abbess of Sta. Marina
told me that she with her religious had a purpose
that the night that the body rested in their
church to have stolen it out and to have stuffed
the coffin with some other matter, alleging that
it was proper to them, and that her body, who
was the foundress, should remain in her own
church, and it was against reason they should be
deprived of so holy a treasure so due to them. I
answered that we had the key of the coffin; and
the lock broken, it would have been perceived;
and withal it had broken her last will and desire
and would have procured much scandal and

debate; nor could I permit it, being one of the executors. "The lock seen, and the consideration thereof did only stay us, said she."

There served no reply to the abbess of Sta. Clara but she would see the body; nor would she sign nor agree to anything before she saw it, although it was fast locked and no breech at all to be seen in the coffin which, upon the boards, was covered close with black velvet, laced on the sides and ends, thick nailed with gilded nails, and double hinges fast nailed at all the corners gilded. So, to give contentment to their curiosity, the coffin was opened and the face seen, which was twelve days after her death, still remaining fair, so seemly and sweet and with so lively colours, as if she had been living; her hands tender, flexible and white, as they were while she lived. And out of her nostrils dropped a little blood, so fair, fresh and red, as if it had been from a lamb; which a priest standing there took in his handkerchief, although her body had not been opened, (for she did precisely command in her testament, charging her executors that no person should touch nor come near her body until her women had shrouded it up,) nor been dressed with spices, balms nor other drugs; so as all that saw it stood admired and might say: "*Laudabilis Deus in sanctis suis.*"

The next morning, being Saturday the 4th of February, the exequies of her funeral were to be solemnized, which continued from six o'clock in the morning to four in the evening. For first the Recollects of St. Francis's Order did sing their Nocturn and Mass so solemn as their Order may permit, with a Responsory after, sprinkling holy water and incensing about the monument. After them the Dominicans did the same also, more solemnly. After them the Franciscans did the like, the Superior still singing the Mass. Then next, the priests of the great church, the dean doing the office; the Nocturn sung and Mass celebrated most solemnly; and at the end of Mass they sung *Alternis vicibus*, five responsories, five times sprinkled, and five times incensed, about the monument. After them the nuns of the same church began their office, and after they had sung their nocturn, High Mass was celebrated; after the gospel whereof had been sung, was preached a sermon by the Prior of the Dominicans. His theme was out of the 114th Psalm, "Convertere anima mea in requiem tuam, quia Dominus beneficit tibi. Quia eripuit animam meam de morte, oculos meos a lacrymis, pedes meos a lapsu. Placebo Domino in regione vivorum;" which he applied very learnedly and divinely to the person, life and death of our duchess.

After this office was done, as the former had been, they took down the coffin to be carried down into the cave, where many other bodies lay in chests that were of the blood and descendants of the house of Feria. I was one who assisted to bear her body into that vault, which gave no offence, but with as good a savour as might be wished, was there deposed, "*ut in resurrectionis gloria inter sanctos et electos resuscitata respiret.*" Nine days after we stayed there, assisting daily at the sung Mass, which was in the church of Sta. Clara; so commanded by her Grace's will, and the ninth day the solemnity was more than ordinary.

The house of our Duchess, as she had ordered by will, remained two months, every servant there having their allowance as when she lived, to have that time to provide themselves. Presently upon our return, all legacies were paid; and before the two months were expired, all dues for Masses and other alms were discharged, and the annuities bequeathed so settled as all future questions were prevented that might hinder the due payment.

I should describe here the outward habit and constitution of the body and stature of the Duchess, which is in the history distinctly noted as she grew in years; and when I came to her service in the year 1603, in the first year of King James, she was in the sixty-sixth year of her age; which together with the heats of Spain, was much extenuated, beginning a little to stoop. She was somewhat higher than ordinary; of a comely person, a lively aspect, a gracious countenance, very clear-skinned, quick in senses; for she had her sight and hearing to her last hour. Until she broke her arm, she was perfect in all parts; her person venerable and with majesty; all showed a nobility and did win a reverent respect from all. I have not seen of her age a more fair, comely and respectful personage; which was perfected with modest comportment, deep judgment, graceful humility and true piety. Of her may be notably and really spoken those praises which are expressed in Holy Scripture of a Good Woman.

INDEX.

BOOKS FOR MEDITATION
AND RETREAT.

————

1. THE CHRISTIAN REFORMED IN MIND AND MANNERS. By Father Benedict Rogacci, S.J. 7s. 6d.

2. PIOUS AFFECTIONS TOWARDS GOD AND THE SAINTS. (Meditations for every day in the Year.) By Father Nicolas Lancicius, S.J. One Vol. 7s. 6d.

3. THE LIFE AND TEACHING OF JESUS CHRIST. Arranged in Meditations for every day in the year. By Father Nicolas Avancino, S.J. Two Vols. 10s. 6d.

————

BIOGRAPHIES.

————

LIFE AND LETTERS OF ST. FRANCIS XAVIER. By the Rev. H. J. Coleridge. Two Vols. 15s.
A cheaper edition in one Vol. 9s.

LIFE AND LETTERS OF ST. TERESA. By the same. Vols. I. and II. 15s. (Vol. III. in preparation.)

CHRONICLE OF ST. ANTONY OF PADUA. 3s. 6d.

STORY OF ST. STANISLAUS KOSTKA. 3s. 6d.

LIFE OF THE BLESSED JOHN BERCHMANS. By Father Goldie. 6s.

————

LONDON: BURNS AND OATES.

BIOGRAPHIES—*(Continued)*.

LIFE OF CHRISTOPHER COLUMBUS. By Rev. A. Knight. 5s.

LIFE OF THE VEN. CLAUDE DE LA COLOMBIERE. 5s.

ENGLISH CARMELITE LIVES:

1. LIFE OF MOTHER CATHARINE BURTON. New Edition. 6s.

2. LIFE OF MOTHER MARGARET MOSTYN. New Edition 6s.

A GRACIOUS LIFE. (Mdme. Acarie) By E. Bowles. 6s.

LIFE OF ST. THOMAS OF HEREFORD. 6s.

DURING THE PERSECUTION. Autobiography of Father John Gerard, S.J. From the original Latin, by the Rev. G. R. Kingdon, S.J. 5s.

GASTON DE SEGUR. Condensed from the French Memoir by the Marquis de Segur. 3s. 6d.

LIFE OF LADY FALKLAND. By Lady G. Fullerton. 5s.

LIFE OF MOTHER MARY TERESA BALL. By Rev. H. J. Coleridge (with portrait). 7s. 6d.

LIFE OF MARY WARD. By M. C. E. Chambers, of the Institute of the Blessed Virgin. Edited by the Rev. H. J. Coleridge, S. J. 2 Vols, each 7s. 6d.

ST. MARY'S CONVENT, YORK. (History of the Convent). 7s. 6d.

LIFE OF JANE DORMER, DUCHESS OF FERIA. Immediately.

LONDON: BURNS AND OATES.

WORKS ON THE LIFE OF OUR LORD.

BY THE

REV. H. J. COLERIDGE.

———

1. THE LIFE OF OUR LIFE. Two Vols. 15s.

2. THE WORKS AND WORDS OF OUR SAVIOUR. One Vol. 7s. 6d.

3. THE STORY OF THE GOSPELS. One Vol. 7s. 6d.

THE HOLY INFANCY. Three Volumes. 7s. 6d. each. Together 20s.

    1. THE PREPARATION OF THE INCARNATION.

    2. THE NINE MONTHS. Our Lord's Life in the Womb.

    3. THE THIRTY YEARS. The Infancy and Hidden Life of Our Lord.

THE PUBLIC LIFE OF OUR LORD. Ten Volumes are now published:

    1. THE MINISTRY OF ST. JOHN BAPTIST.

    2. THE PREACHING OF THE BEATITUDES (First Part of the Sermon on the Mount.)

    3. THE SERMON ON THE MOUNT (Second Part).

    4. THE SERMON ON THE MOUNT (Third Part).

    5. THE TRAINING OF THE APOSTLES (Part I.).

    6. THE TRAINING OF THE APOSTLES (Part II.).

    7. THE TRAINING OF THE APOSTLES (Part III.).

    8. THE TRAINING OF THE APOSTLES (Part IV.).

———

LONDON: BURNS AND OATES.

WORKS ON THE LIFE OF OUR LORD—
(*Continued*).

_____

9. THE PREACHING OF THE CROSS (Part I.).

10. THE PREACHING OF THE CROSS. (Part II.).
(Immediately.)

6s. 6d. each Volume.

_____

By the same.

THE RETURN OF THE KING. Discourses on the Latter
Days. 7s. 6d.

THE BAPTISM OF THE KING. Considerations on the
Sacred Passion. 7s. 6d.

THE PRISONERS OF THE KING. Thoughts on the
Catholic Doctrine of Purgatory. New Edition
3s. 6d.

_____

WORKS ON OUR BLESSED LADY.

_____

1. THE MOTHER OF THE KING. Mary during
the Life of our Lord. 7s. 6d.

2. THE MOTHER OF THE CHURCH. Mary
during the First Apostolic Age.

(Third Volume in Preparation.)

_____

Edited by the same.

THE HISTORY OF THE SACRED PASSION. By Father
Louis de la Palma. 7s. 6d. A cheap Edition, 5s.

THE HOURS OF THE PASSION. From the Latin of
Lindolph the Saxon. 7s. 6d.

THE SEVEN WORDS ON THE CROSS. By Cardinal
Bellarmine. 5s.

_____

LONDON: BURNS AND OATES.